I0746648

The Biker's
BELOVED
NAT LOGAN

BROKEN HEARTS
BREWING COMPANY
"Love Is Just a Sip Away"

DEDICATION

This book is about love and happily ever afters with the one you love. I wouldn't be on this journey if it wasn't for the man who swept me off my feet in 1988. He's the one who makes every day better and always told me that I could do this. We'll be celebrating our 34th wedding anniversary this year and I'm looking forward to many more. Thank you for believing that I could.

CONTENTS

CHAPTER ONE

Rachel Smithson breathed a sigh of relief at seeing the sign for Bluff Creek, Kansas. They had only twenty more miles to go.

She'd banked their future on this town and the people of the Bluff Creek Brotherhood MC, all because of the sweet woman she'd met first online in a crafting forum, and later in person, who had said Rachel could find a home. When Clara had traveled to a craft show where Rachel had a booth to meet in person, Rachel hadn't known what Clara had planned. But Clara was one of those people who inspired trust. It was the only thing to explain what Rachel had done.

Rachel wasn't usually impulsive, but circumstances dictated that she take a chance on a woman she barely knew. But just like she always did,

Rachel would put a smile on her face and look at all the positives. Frowning or grouching about circumstances never changed them; it only made the situation harder to get through.

She glanced behind her, seeing the greatest gifts in her life and her whole world. Whether it was raining or the sun was shining, each day was brighter because her kids were in it. And if this worked out the way Rachel hoped, her kids would have a stable environment for school and get to know friends.

Michelle, her youngest, had so wanted to stay awake to see the town but had given in to sleep a couple hours ago. Her little man had covered his sister with a blanket and made sure she was comfortable and safe in the vehicle. Well, vehicle and home in one. She'd designed and built it herself as a home away from home at craft shows. But now, it was their home, and she was so thankful for it. It had beds for all of them, a stove, microwave, sink, refrigerator, toilet, and a really small shower. She'd added an outdoor shower for the summer that had sides she could pull out from the opened back doors along with a curtain.

Her little man, Marcus, wasn't going to sleep until she had them set up. Despite being only nine, he acted so much older. The promise in Bluff Creek of him getting to be a kid was one of the many things that had her grabbing onto Clara's offer with both hands.

She'd told the kids they were going on an adventure, and both of them had smiled and asked where they were going. She was thankful for the resilience of her kids and their smiling faces. She had her kids, and that meant, no matter the circumstances, everything would be okay.

She had her crafts to sell, and Clara had promised the Bluff Creek MC had a job for her in addition to her crafts if she wanted. They had a place to live. She had a job, and Clara had guaranteed that food would be provided as part of her pay. Rachel thanked her lucky stars that she and Clara had connected.

She drove down what she assumed was Main Street. She saw the businesses that Clara had mentioned: Bluff Creek Ink, Regina's Roadside Refuge, and Bluff Creek Crafts. Broken Hearts Brewing was supposed to be right after that, along with the MC's K9 training and rescue. She couldn't remember what Clara had called it.

The last two weeks had been a whirlwind, so Rachel was giving herself some grace for not remembering everything.

Rachel only hoped that Clara wasn't irritated with her because Rachel wasn't going by the compound like Clara had directed. She was two days early. Once she'd made the decision and their life had changed, she'd gotten them on the road. With how kind the MC was being, Rachel couldn't bring herself to barge in early and expect them to be ready.

She would park behind the coffee shop and set up their van. They could explore the town tomorrow and then go by the MC. Two in the morning was not the time to barge in on an MC compound. At least that's what Rachel assumed.

Clara spoke about the MC as if it were a big family. Rachel's only interactions with an MC had been reading about them in romance books or watching shows on TV.

"Is this it?" Marcus asked, his voice a little husky from fighting sleep.

She nodded, "Yep, buddy, it's our new start."

"I'm excited. Clara said there are kids my age," he said softly, keeping his voice down so he wouldn't wake his sister.

She made the turn into the parking lot and decided she'd pull around so they were underneath the light in the lot. She had to maneuver a little to get the small trailer attached to the van straight. She'd had one on her wish list to be able to bring more crafts to events, but when their circumstances changed, she'd bought the small trailer to have room for some of their items that wouldn't fit in the van.

She had an awning she'd installed on the passenger side of the van for them to have some shade from the early morning sun, but there was no reason to put it out tonight. She'd put up the window coverings to keep the sun out and do the minimum things. Her shoulders ached. Her eyes were dry and itchy, and she didn't think she could deal with all the things she normally did to make the van seem like home.

It had been an eventful two weeks, but she wasn't going to think about that tonight. Nope—not tonight.

She needed sleep in the worst way, and she was going to go to sleep knowing she had a plan and the promise of a future in Bluff Creek. She scooted between the seats into the main area of the van. She and Marcus efficiently transformed the van into their bedroom. She installed her metal guards that would keep anyone out, even if they broke the van's windows. She turned the two front seats toward each other and added the items she'd made to have a bed for Michelle. Lifting her daughter, she moved her, tucking the blanket around her with her favorite little stuffed animal.

Marcus took care of making the couch into his bed while she did the same with her sleeping area, lowering it from the ceiling. She plugged the nightlight in just in case anyone needed the bathroom during the night, taking her turn after Marcus got changed and brushed his teeth.

Once he was settled under his blanket with all types of motorcycles on it, she leaned over and kissed his forehead. "I love you, buddy. I'm excited for tomorrow. How about we eat pancakes at the restaurant in town?"

His eyes lit up. He hadn't had much to smile about lately but pancakes were a winner.

"Clara said they are delicious and that you can get toppings. Will she meet us?" he asked. Clara had quickly won over both her kids with her kind demeanor and loving manner. With everything that had happened, the promise of seeing Clara had been a beacon for the kids to focus on.

"We'll see. Let's play it by ear, but we'll definitely call her and see about meeting," Rachel replied.

She walked over to her bed, tugging the light cover back and crawling under it. Her arms, shoulders, and the back of her neck ached from the long drive, but she wasn't going to get back up to take any medicine or find her heating pad. She was exhausted and was positive she'd fall asleep quickly. The quiet of the little town soothed something in Rachel as she closed her eyes, breathing deeply.

Tomorrow was the first day of a whole new life.

CHAPTER TWO

G unner Adams took the turn onto Main Street and headed toward his new obsession—Broken Hearts Brewing Company. When he'd met his brother Flick in Texas to help Flick and his girlfriend with an issue the club was having, he had no idea he'd end up getting to have one of his dreams fulfilled—to own and run a coffee shop. He grinned in the early morning light. The sun was just peeking over the horizon, and the cool, crisp January morning had Gunner glad he'd added a long sleeve shirt under his cut.

He always ran a little hot, and once he got busy in the kitchen of Broken Hearts, he'd probably switch into a short sleeve. Ovens running and the coffee perking would warm up the area.

He backed his bike into a slot in front of the building. Sure, he had parking available in the back but there was something about unlocking the front door and walking into his dream that settled something inside him.

Gunner had followed in his older brother Brody's footsteps and joined the military right out of high school. Between money being tight and Gunner not being sure exactly what he wanted to do with his life, he decided to serve. Not only did he have a purpose to serve his country, but how hard could it be if Brody, his tight-ass rule-following older brother, could do it?

Gunner chuckled, glancing around the main room of the shop, wondering how he could have been so naïve about the military. Gunner could smile about it now, but his time at boot camp was brutal. He was sure it was hard for everyone, but Gunner had been the prankster in high school. He'd wanted to make everyone smile because he would never live up to his oldest brother's perfect behavior. And where his friends in high school had enjoyed his antics, the Army, well—not so much.

Now, almost thirty years from when he showed up for boot camp, he could appreciate how far he'd come. He still enjoyed a good prank, but they had their time and place.

The warm wood floor had some dust streaks. After they'd mopped it every day and the workmen just dirtied it up, he'd decided to mop every three days. The tables, chairs, and couches were being delivered next week. Gunner was waiting for the craftsmen to finish the bookcases and the display cabinet for the food items. There were so many steps, but Gunner didn't get stressed by it. His excitement overwhelmed any little irritants that came up.

He'd always known that he enjoyed cooking and baking. He was the son who was in the kitchen with his mom, learning all her tips and tricks. But until he heard his now sister-in-law with her idea for Broken Hearts Brewing Company, he hadn't known what was next. Her concept had sent anticipation zinging through him.

Cooking and baking for people gave Gunner a sense of satisfaction. The smile on someone's face as they bit into a scone or hummed while savoring his dishes sent a wave of joy through him. It was truly one of those times when his giving of a gift brought him as much delight as the person receiving his creation.

He'd be forever grateful to the Bluff Creek Brotherhood MC for letting it be his baby. In the six months since he'd been here, he'd formed deep bonds with the men of the MC. Besides his brothers Flick and Brody, he'd enjoyed getting to know both the Originals and his generation. And the women surprised him with how they wove each person who came to Bluff Creek into the fabric of the Bluff Creek family. He was fond of all of them, and he shouldn't have favorites, but Regina, Meg, and Clara were the women he went to most.

Bluff Creek was a family and he and Brody had soaked it up. At first, he and Brody had lived with his brother Flick and his wife, Beth, at her insistence. It had helped while Brody recovered from his injuries and allowed the brothers to spend time together. But right after Christmas, he and Brody had moved into the clubhouse. They'd needed their own place, and they'd wanted to give Flick and Beth their alone time.

Clara had come to him about hiring a crafter she'd met. The woman was going to make some of the crocheted items the women had come up with for people with broken hearts, whether it was through widowhood or a breakup. Clara's friend was also going to be in charge of ordering the books and organizing some specialty nights. After listening to Clara sing her praises, he'd brought it up in council that if she took that much off his plate, then she'd be a good assistant manager. He had the go-ahead to work with her and to up her position and salary if she lived up to Clara's praises.

Broken Hearts Brewing was going to be the place you could go to fill your stomach with good food and drink but also to heal your heart.

Gunner snickered, glancing toward the hall-way that led to one of Beth's ideas to *heal your heart*. Grief had cycles and anger was the first.

Their *Broken Hearts Smash Room* would allow the grieving person to work out their anger by destroying a multitude of items. He'd had to do research to ensure they followed all guidelines with the room hooked onto their coffee brewing and food handling area. With soundproofed walls and two doors people had to go through for cleaning up, Gunner was positive they'd pass any safety issues. Gunner didn't want the participants tracking glass and small metal pieces into the coffee shop. When it was ready, individuals would change into different shoes, put on overalls, protective glasses, and a hairnet to go work out their frustrations. Gunner thought he and his brothers would have benefited from a room like that when they lost their mom.

Their soft opening was two days before Valentine's Day on the 12th, which was exactly four weeks from today. His assistant manager was supposed to be in town two days from now on Saturday, January 10th, and he couldn't wait to meet her. He'd jotted some ideas down, but they'd have to wait until he met her in person.

He flicked the lights on in the kitchen, started the ovens, and went to the sink to wash his hands. He glanced out the windows he'd had added over the sink to allow some natural light in. He loved being in the kitchen, but so many restaurants had windowless kitchens. With the Broken Hearts kitchen being completely enclosed from the front of the shop other than a swinging door, he wanted a way to see the outside.

A van was parked in the back lot under the streetlight. Rachel's Crafty Creations was painted on the side of the bright yellow van in a multitude of colors. He smiled just seeing the pretty lettering. It seemed his crafty person was as excited about getting here as he was to have her.

He glanced at his watch. Seven-thirty in the morning and Gunner was hungry. He could go ahead and start trying out some more recipes. But the part of him that had been welcomed to Bluff Creek wouldn't let him just go back to baking. He'd check on them and see if anyone was up. He could either make them breakfast or take them across to Regina's.

He headed out the back door. As he got closer, he could hear sounds from inside the van. He rapped on the metal door, calling out as he did because the last thing he wanted to do was scare Rachel.

"Hey, I'm Gunner, the manager of Broken Hearts Brewing. Welcome to Bluff Creek. I was wondering if I could fix you breakfast," Gunner said.

The clicking of the locks being disengaged sounded loud in the cool morning. The door opened and Gunner just stared.

Fuck him. He was going to have to work with this smiling beauty who looked like she was filled with liquid sunshine. How would he survive?

"Good morning," the woman said. Gunner loved the wide smile she had, but spotting two small kids behind her, he was also now curious. Clara hadn't mentioned the woman was married.

"I'm Rachel and we'd love to do breakfast. Marcus was wanting pancakes at the diner because Clara raved about them, but I don't want to say no if you want to fix them," Rachel's melodic voice wrapped around Gunner. He barely controlled a shiver at her words.

"Oh, then we definitely have to go to the diner for pancakes. They are the best. Marcus, I'm Gunner. Nice to meet you," Gunner said, holding his hand out to Marcus.

After Marcus glared at him, Gunner had to wonder what was going on besides just meeting a new person.

"Marcus," Rachel admonished.

Marcus stuck out his hand. When Gunner grasped his, Marcus squeezed as hard as he could. It seemed as if Marcus was letting Gunner know he wasn't a pushover. Gunner had no idea why Marcus felt he needed to, but Gunner was letting him have the win without getting him in trouble with his mom.

"You've got a strong grip, Marcus. I could use you if you ever want to come help me knead dough sometime," Gunner said, with a smile.

"Mom, I need to go," Marcus said, raising his eyebrows at her.

"Oh, well, let me get dressed and we'll get out," Rachel said.

"If you want a private bathroom, Marcus, the coffee shop has the restrooms done. You'd need shoes because I didn't sweep after the workmen left yesterday," Gunner offered.

"Can I, Mom?" Marcus said, bouncing on his toes.

"Sure," she said, handing him his shoes to slip on.

Gunner led Marcus through the kitchen and left him in the bathroom after making sure the stalls had toilet paper.

Gunner spent his time staring out at the van where the woman who had knocked him off-kilter was getting ready. The visceral reaction he had to her had never happened before with anyone. He'd been attracted to women, but this was different. He rubbed at the strange ache in his chest and down his abdomen.

"I'm done," Marcus said.

Gunner turned around and grinned. "It's nice to have some privacy, isn't it?"

Marcus rolled his eyes. "Everybody poops but every time, Michelle has to comment how it smells or about any fart sounds. She's annoying."

Gunner chuckled. "Yep, I get you. I have an older brother and a younger brother. My older brother was perfect. And my younger brother could make friends with anyone. It's hard having siblings sometimes. But when you need them, they've got your back."

Marcus seemed to be considering his words but was stopped from replying when Rachel and Michelle came into the kitchen.

"Is it pancake time? I'm Michelle, but Mom and Marcus call me Chelle. Are you nice? If you are, you can call me Chelle too," she said, grinning at Gunner, with a gap where she was missing a front tooth. Both kids resembled their mom in looks.

Did it make him weird that he wanted to protect both of them from ever being hurt?

"I think I'm nice, but maybe you should ask Clara. I know she'd tell the truth," Gunner replied. He wasn't taking her question lightly. Her question, coupled with Marcus' behavior, had

Gunner worrying about what had happened to them before they came to Bluff Creek.

"Who is ready for pancakes? I'm starving," Rachel said, smiling and making faces at her kids. The joy radiating from this woman made him want to soak it all in.

Gunner led them through the front of the shop, with Rachel oohing and aahing about how she couldn't wait to get started. Seeing her excitement increased his own. This shop was going to be such a fun space when they were done. They reached the quiet street out front; Rachel grabbed both kids' hands and skipped across the street, the little kids' giggles bringing a smile to his face.

"Skip with me, Gunner," Michelle called, and darned if he could tell her no.

He grasped her hand and skipped across the street with the kids. He stepped ahead to open the door for them to the diner, waiting for all three to go in before following. He stifled his groan at the look of Rachel's butt cupped in her jeans. She was a tiny thing, only coming to his shoulders. Gunner was six foot three, and she made him think of a pixie when she stood beside him.

"We can sit at the table with the reserved sign. It's for anyone connected with the MC," Gunner said, leading the family over to the table and helping Michelle move her chair closer.

CHAPTER THREE

Rachel breathed a sigh of relief. It seemed like she could relax now that they were here and had been welcomed by so many people. Right as their pancakes were delivered, Clara walked in with Beth and Flick.

Michelle and Marcus immediately ran into her arms for hugs. After the hugs, Clara introduced Gunner's brother and his wife, Beth, who had come up with the idea for Broken Hearts Brewing.

The kids had eaten and chatted with the adults, soaking up the attention from someone besides their mom. Rachel agreed that Clara was right. The fluffy pancakes, crispy bacon, and scrambled eggs had been perfect.

"Well, who do we have here?" a man in one of the Bluff Creek vest thingies said. His vest said his name was Dex. She wondered if it stood for anything.

"Hey, Dex, this is Rachel and her children, Marcus and Michelle. Rachel is going to be helping out at Broken Hearts," Beth said.

"It's nice to meet you all. I need to grab the take-out for the gun range. Welcome to Bluff Creek," Dex said, walking away.

He wasn't unfriendly but him almost running away was a little strange.

"Now that everyone's almost done with breakfast, do you want to explore the town, or would you like to get your stuff moved into your house?" Clara asked.

"Our house, please, Mom," Michelle and Marcus said.

She grinned at their excitement. "I think that sounds perfect."

"How about Flick, Beth, and I take the kids with us? Gunner, can you drive Rachel to the compound?" Clara said.

Rachel wasn't sure how she felt about her kids being out of her sight, but if this truly was going to be their home, then she needed to relax the reins a little.

"Sure. Are you all right with that, Rachel?" Gunner asked.

Was she all right being in her van where there was a fold-down bed six feet away from the tall, rugged, tattooed biker? No, but she wasn't sure how she could articulate the fear she now lived with. Rachel was barely five foot three and Gunner was easily a foot taller than she was. She'd lost a lot of weight over the last couple of months, and she definitely didn't have any muscle tone. If he wasn't a good guy, she wouldn't stand a chance against him. She didn't know enough about him yet to know if she could trust him.

Rachel cleared her throat, which had gone dry at the thought of being alone with Gunner in her van, and croaked out, "Sure."

"We'll be about fifteen minutes behind you if that's okay. I'm sure Rachel wants to see the space so she can start deciding how to display items," Gunner suggested.

Despite knowing she'd be leaving her kids alone a little longer, Gunner was right. Rachel was itching to see the space. She'd had ideas tumbling around her head since Clara had given her the offer of a job. Now to see if they'd work in the space provided.

So many fun things she could do, and, hopefully, Gunner would accept her ideas and not discount them because she was a woman.

The kids jumped up to go with Clara, but Rachel pulled them aside for a minute.

"I want you to enjoy your time, but no fighting between you two. You treat your sibling like they are a new friend you just met and want to impress them with your behavior, got it?" Rachel said, making sure her face was conveying the severity of her request. Rarely did the kids see her not smiling, but their fights could be epic and today was not the day for Bluff Creek to be introduced to them.

"We promise we'll be good," Marcus said, grinning at her. She hoped the mischief shining in his eyes was from excitement and not something he was planning to irritate his sister.

"Yep, we'll be good," Michelle said, her body wiggling in excitement.

"Okay, love you and listen to Clara, Beth, and Flick," Rachel gave one last direction before watching her kids walk out the door.

"They'll be fine—spoiled rotten probably but fine," Gunner said.

Following Gunner across the street, Rachel had her first good look at Broken Hearts Brewing in the daylight. The building's bricks were painted a bright white. A large pink and red heart logo was painted on the upper level of the building. Inside the heart shape was a red and pink drawing of an anatomical heart. A ribbon ran across the heart with Broken Hearts Brewing Company lettered underneath with the phrase *"Love Is Just a Sip Away."* The bottom level of the building had white brick decorated with pink and red hearts that went up about four feet. The rest of the building had huge windows. A large pink and red striped awning extended over the front of the store.

Gunner opened the door, holding it open for her. Her first glimpse of the space had her catching her breath. It was exactly what she'd hoped for. Warm wood floors with one wall being floor-to-ceiling bookcases. Display areas along the back were just waiting to be filled.

"The furniture will be coming soon. Sofas, coffee tables, comfy chairs to read and relax in, along with some regular dining tables. The only things set in stone are the food display cases and the built-in bookshelves. We can discuss where you think things might go, but if, once it's set up, we realize we need to move things, we can. This is a learning experience. Back here," Gunner said, walking toward a hallway. "This is the smash room, bathrooms, and this door is to the staircase for upstairs, which is currently extra storage. It's been painted and has wood floors, so it's available if we need to expand at some point."

He opened a second door. "This is the employee area along with storage for items. I'm open to whatever you think about all the areas."

Rachel couldn't keep from smiling. This was better than she dreamed. She was ready to dig in and get things set up.

"Let's head over to the compound and get you settled in your house. The workmen are supposed to completely finish today, which means we can sweep and wet mop and not worry whether stock we put out will get dirty after today."

Gunner's smile had her reminding herself that this was a new place and everything looked fine, but she'd learned over time that not everything was as it seemed. She'd wait to relax and trust everyone once they'd earned it.

CHAPTER FOUR

R achel kissed Marcus' forehead. "I love you, buddy. Sleep well."

"I will, Mom. I like it here. And did you see the big fence they have around the property? No one's getting in," Marcus said, closing his eyes.

Oh, the innocence of children. Rachel did love the tall fence surrounding the property, but she didn't know everyone who lived here. How could she trust them if she didn't know them?

Clara, along with what could only be termed as an abundance of people, had helped move all their personal belongings into the house. When Regina, Clara's friend, had realized that Rachel had two children and did crafts, she changed which house Rachel and the kids were going to live in. She walked them two houses down to one that had three bedrooms, a full basement, and a loft that Regina thought would be perfect for all Rachel's crafts. She had to admit it was a lovely space. And because it was hidden from people walking in, if she wanted to leave things out while she worked on them, she could.

Multiple kids had shown up to play with Marcus and Chelle. Rachel had tried to keep track of the names but had given up. Between the adults and kids, she'd met at least fifty new people today.

Her refrigerator was filled with some meals that could be heated up to eat, and her pantry was stocked with all the necessities. Every need she'd had, they'd taken care of.

Her only embarrassment, besides how little they had, was when Phoebe had asked Michelle where her toys were. Michelle had piped up that her bad daddy had sold their toys. The silence in the house was deafening. Rachel had only hoped that no one would ask any questions. She needed just one day when she didn't have to think about the kids' dad.

But no one had asked questions. In under an hour, though, toys for both the kids had shown up.

Rachel walked around the house checking the doors and windows before glancing into Michelle's room. She'd fallen asleep almost before she'd finished her bath.

Today had been exciting and busy. Rachel was ready to relax, and she relaxed best by crafting. She brewed a cup of hot tea and took it upstairs.

She looked around the room. Everything had a place, and she could easily find whatever she needed.

She set her drink down on the table beside the comfortable rocking recliner Clara had insisted she needed.

Gunner and his brothers had wrestled the chair up the stairs into the loft. She had giggled along with everyone else as they tried to get it through the wooden banister separating the loft from below, the wall, and a bookcase that was built in directly by the stairs.

Flick yelling *Pivot* had them all laughing. Brody, the brother she'd nicknamed the broody one in her head, had waited until they were done and were walking down the stairs. He'd been behind Flick and had given him a kick in the behind, sending him tumbling down the stairs. Gunner had just chuckled and shaken his head at them.

She picked up the pale pink yarn and her crochet needle. She'd sold out at the last craft show of a couple of the items she wanted to show Gunner. The pink loaf cat was part of her idea for gift boxes for people who visited Broken Hearts. She also wondered about having them available to ship to people if someone asked. She needed to write down her ideas after she finished this little one because she'd thought of a lot of ideas on the drive.

She lost herself in the motions of crocheting. She breathed deeply and relaxed. They were safe behind walls tonight. Tomorrow she'd meet with Gunner and they could talk ideas about the shop.

She finished the cat in under an hour. She'd become faster the more she made. She stared at the pink one and then had an idea. She looked through the craft supplies she'd brought into the house.

Darn it!

She wanted a purple and a soft buttery yellow for her two ideas. She'd only brought a small amount of yarn into the house. She glanced down at her thin T-shirt and sleep shorts. It was chilly outside, but the house was toasty warm.

The kids were safe inside. She could run out to her van parked in the driveway. She had debated about parking in the garage when Gunner had offered. If she had, she wouldn't have needed to go outside. But that small part of her that wasn't quite ready to trust had wanted the van and trailer outside to be able to make a quick getaway if needed.

She pulled her curtain on the window closest to where her van was parked and looked outside. She didn't see anyone. She grabbed the house keys so she could get back inside. She opened her front door and stepped out. Locking the door, she hurried toward the van. The chilly night air had her nipples tightening and Rachel shivering. Opening the van door, she found her yarn divided by color and grabbed the small totes with purple and yellow. She started to leave, then thought about how she felt and how mad she was about her situation.

She bent down and crawled under the table area where she'd stored the tote of black yarn. She started scooting backward from under the table, pulling the tote.

"Everything okay?" Gunner's voice called.

She jerked, slamming her head into the table and yelping.

She backed out, tears filling her eyes, and sat up to check her head where she hit it.

"Oh crap. I'm so sorry. I didn't mean to startle you. I was taking a walk on the compound and saw a light on in your van. I was worried it got left on and would drain the battery. Then I heard someone rummaging in it," he said, his voice close by.

She turned, her face flushing. "I just hit my head. I had an idea and needed some yarn," she said, waving her hand toward the totes.

"I feel horrible you hit your head because I startled you. Can I at least carry them for you?" he asked.

Rachel stared at Gunner's face. Unlike the kids' father, Gunner's face expressed everything he was feeling—regret at her getting hurt and a need to help her.

"I'd appreciate that," she said. She pushed the totes toward him and used the counter to steady herself as she stood.

"Whoa, you look a little unsteady. Are you sure you're okay?" he asked.

She took a deep breath and took stock. Her head ached, and her fingers had a little blood from when she checked her head. She wasn't sure why she felt off.

"I think I'm okay," she said, Gunner's face wavering in front of her.

He dropped the totes and then everything went dark.

Gunner dropped the totes and reached for Rachel, catching her as she fainted. Holding her against him, he texted Stella and Flick for help. He lifted her, grabbing her keys off the cabinet to get back into the house. Once he knew she was okay, he'd come out and get the totes.

"Everything okay?" Stone called.

"Rachel hit her head when I startled her. Can you unlock the door and then bring these totes in?" Gunner asked, tossing him the keys. Lifting Rachel in his arms, he realized how thin she was. She had a beautiful face, but the shadows under her eyes and the hollowness below her cheeks worried him.

He carried her in, laying her on the couch in the front room. He'd move her to the bedroom if Stella or Flick said to, but he wasn't encroaching on her personal space without her okay.

"What did you do to my mommy?" Marcus yelled before he pushed Gunner away and started beating on Gunner wherever his hands could reach. "You're supposed to be nice, Clara said. Not like our bad daddy!" Marcus screamed.

Gunner held up his hands and let Marcus get it all out. When Gunner didn't fight back or try to grab Marcus, he paused and stared up at Gunner.

"I think you're a brave boy for defending your mom. I'm not a bad man. Your mom was getting totes from underneath the table, and I asked a question. It surprised her..."

"Oh, did she hit her head on the latch? I've done that a couple times, and it really hurts," Marcus said, wiping his nose and the tears seeping out of his eyes.

"Yes. Flick and Stella are going to come check her out to make sure she's okay," Gunner said, slowly moving his hand to Marcus' shoulder. He wanted to comfort the kid, but this outburst told him there might be more to their story he needed to be aware of.

Marcus didn't flinch when Gunner placed his hand on Marcus' shoulder. Marcus moved closer and leaned against Gunner.

"Can I tell you a secret?" Marcus asked, staring up at Gunner.

Gunner nodded and knelt down so Marcus was face to face with him.

"You can, but if you're in danger, I need to share it with your mommy," Gunner said.

Marcus leaned closer, wrapping his arms around Gunner's neck and burying his face against Gunner's chest.

"Daddy said if I told, he'd kill Mommy and Chelle," Marcus whispered.

Stone knelt down beside them. "You can trust Gunner and all of us. We won't let your daddy do that."

Gunner pushed the rage he felt at Marcus' words deep down inside. He didn't want Marcus to feel how angry he was.

"What does he not want you to tell?" Gunner asked, breathing deeply, his arms wrapped around Marcus. He reminded himself that the kids and Rachel were both safe here at Bluff Creek.

"I saw him pushing a needle in his arm," Marcus said softly. Gunner had to strain to make out what he said. A needle in his arm—had Rachel's husband been a drug user the whole time, or had it been something new? The small amount of time he'd been around Rachel, he didn't see her being okay with drugs being around her children.

"All right, where's the patient?" Flick said, walking in with Stella.

"Mommy's here. She hit her head on the hard metal thing under the table. It hurts when it happens," Marcus said, turning toward Flick.

"Well, let's see how she is," Flick said.

Gunner kept his arm around Marcus as Flick and Stella checked her over. Rachel moaned a little as she came to.

"Hey, Rachel. Do you remember me?" Flick asked.

Rachel nodded, then grabbed her head.

"You're Beth's husband," she said.

Flick chuckled. "Yes, I am Beth's husband. I'm also an EMT, and Stella here is a nurse practitioner. Does anything else besides your head hurt?"

Gunner listened as Stella and Flick ran through questions regarding Rachel's symptoms. They'd helped her sit up, and Flick had gone to the kitchen, returning with some juice for her to sip.

"Have you been skipping meals?" Stella asked.

"Maybe. I haven't deliberately been skipping meals. I ate breakfast with Gunner and the kids. We've been so busy for the last week, and I haven't been very hungry," Rachel said.

"How's your sleep been?" Flick asked.

"Not great. We've been traveling and I don't sleep deeply in the van," Rachel replied, sipping the juice.

"I think, and I can tell by Flick's face he's coming to the same conclusion, you're exhausted, run down, and didn't take in enough calories today. When you hit your head, I don't believe your body could handle processing the adrenaline. I'd really like you to eat and drink something and see how you feel. Does a smoothie sound good, or would you rather we heated up some of the mac n' cheese with barbecue chicken? We need to make sure you have a good balance of protein with your calories," Stella said.

"I'm not very hungry, but the mac n' cheese sounds better than a smoothie," she said, wrinkling her nose.

Marcus grabbed her hand. Rachel pulled him closer. "I'm okay, buddy."

Marcus nodded and hugged her.

Gunner waited while Flick heated up the food. Stella checked Rachel's pulse. Flick returned with the food and waited until Rachel took her first bite.

Gunner now understood how these men he'd gotten to know could be so upset. Gunner didn't want to stand here helpless. He wanted to wrap Rachel in his arms and fix whatever was wrong with her.

And little Marcus and Chelle. He wanted to make sure their loser of a dad was out of the picture because Gunner wanted to be their dad. He wasn't sure how, in less than twenty-four hours, he'd fallen in love with the woman of his dreams and with her kids.

If Rachel's husband or ex-husband, Gunner wasn't sure which, was available—Gunner would be teaching him a lesson about threatening children. Ripping him apart piece by piece might get rid of the anger Gunner had toward him.

"Rachel, I'd feel better if someone stayed with you tonight. Would it be okay if I slept on your couch? I promise I won't check on you every hour, but I'd like to check on you at least once," Stella said.

Rachel finished chewing her last bite. "Umm, sure, I guess. I think I'm fine, though."

Stella patted her shoulder. "I'm sure you are but I'd like to be sure. Both my girls are living far away, and I know if they'd had this happen, I'd want someone with them overnight."

"Then it's settled. Let's have you stand up and see how steady you are. If everything is good, I'll help you get Marcus settled back in bed and then you," Stella said.

Gunner held out his hand to help Rachel up, and Marcus held his out for her other hand. Gunner hid a smile at Marcus being such a little man. Rachel stood up and seemed steady on her feet.

"All right. We'll shoo the men out except for Marcus. I'd love it if you could get a good eight to ten hours of sleep tonight," Stella said.

"But the shop," Rachel protested.

"Nope. You sleep in. I got a message that the guys are almost done but need at least tomorrow morning to finish. Then I have a crew going in to clean. Tomorrow afternoon at four p.m. is the earliest we can go into the place. Sleep in. Relax. Let me know if you need any food delivered but rest," Gunner said.

Her smile was all the reward he needed.

"Thank you," she said.

Stella led them back to the bedrooms, and Gunner headed toward the door with Stone and Flick. Leaving her was the hardest thing he had to do tonight, but Stella would take care of her.

Rachel and the kids needed to know that they had support from all of Bluff Creek.

Flick patted his back. "Way to be the bigger man. Stella will take care of her, and you can work on winning her heart tomorrow. See ya," Flick said, heading home.

"You okay?" Stone asked.

"I want to tear his father apart piece by piece," Gunner muttered as they walked down the steps.

"I have a key to the gym if you want to go punch something," Stone said.

"Why do you have a key to the gym?"

"Sometimes the only thing that calms me down at night so I can sleep is beating the hell out of something. Locks figured the punching bag at the gym was better than asking the members to let me hit them," Stone said.

Gunner chuckled. He appreciated Locks thinking of them.

"Yep, I think I need that," Gunner said. At least he could expend his anger if he couldn't solve the issue.

CHAPTER FIVE

Gunner threw his arm over his eyes to block the bright sunlight piercing into his brain. Where had he gone to sleep? There wasn't any bright sunlight in his room at the clubhouse.

He lay still, taking stock. His head hurt, and his mouth tasted like he'd dipped it in the farm's manure pile. He stayed still, trying to remember what he'd done.

The smell of brewed coffee tickled his nose. He pulled his arm down and cracked an eye open. Stone held a cup of steaming coffee in front of his face. He accepted it, groaning at the protest his muscles made as he sat up.

"Will you keep quiet? You snored all night. It was like a freight train with asthma was in the room," his brother Brody growled.

He took a sip of the piping hot coffee. It would do. He'd prefer it with one of the many flavored creamers he'd ordered for the shop, but he was just thrilled to have it brought to him.

Gunner took another drink of the coffee. It had cooled down enough so that he could gulp it down. Once he finished, Stone handed him another one.

"We went to the gym last night," Gunner said. Stone nodded.

"I went a little crazy on beating things up," Gunner said.

Stone nodded and left the room. He returned with his own cup of coffee and dropped into the recliner near where Gunner was sitting.

"How'd he get here?" Gunner asked, waving his thumb toward Brody.

"Shut up. I came when Stone texted that he couldn't get you to stop beating on the bag at the gym, and you paid me back by keeping me awake snoring," Brody grumbled.

"You'd think after serving he'd be able to sleep through anything," Gunner said, grinning when Brody uncovered his head to glare.

Gunner thought back over last night. Once Stone had unlocked the gym, they'd put on gloves because Stone said the kids shouldn't see Gunner's hands beat up. They traded some punches, but Gunner had needed more. He'd gone to the heavy bag. Once he started hitting and kicking it, every bit of anger he'd pushed down while listening to Marcus had bubbled up and out.

Stone and Brody had each grabbed an arm when Gunner wouldn't listen to them. His muscles ached, but this morning, he was calm. Calm was what Rachel and the kids deserved.

Stone stood up and grabbed keys off the counter. "Ride to clear your head?"

Gunner nodded. "I'll walk back to the clubhouse, shower, and then be ready. Give me twenty minutes."

Stone nodded.

"Okay, friggin' fine. I'll sleep later. I'm not missing a ride now that my leg is finally strong enough to ride," Brody grumbled, following Gunner out.

Gunner ignored Brody as they walked back. He couldn't get this mad again. Sure, if he saw the jerk who had scared Marcus and hurt Rachel, Gunner would help him see the error of his ways. But for now, he was going to concentrate on showing Rachel the man he was and give her time to trust him.

"Thanks," Gunner mumbled toward his brother.

"No problem. But I think you need to get that snoring fixed before you pursue her. Unless she has earplugs, she won't sleep beside you," Brody said, moving away when Gunner tried to push him.

"I don't snore," Gunner said.

"Yeah, you keep thinking that," Brody said, walking fast to pass Gunner. Gunner sped up, but Brody started running. He wasn't sure why Brody was running, but Gunner was sure that today wasn't going to start with Brody lording it over Gunner that he was older and faster.

They hit the door at the same time and tried to squeeze through together. Regina looked up from the cinnamon rolls she was frosting as they fell into the clubhouse.

"Everything okay?" she asked.

"Yep. Just fine. How are you?" Brody asked, walking over to hug her.

Gunner loved seeing the lighter side of his brother. After Brody had returned injured from overseas, he'd gone through a very grumpy phase. Thank goodness he'd gotten better.

"Good. Rolls are done if you want to eat," Regina offered.

"I need to have a quick shower, and then I'll have one of those," Gunner said.

Regina grinned. "Only one?"

So he might not be able to leave them alone. One was never enough.

"Maybe a couple."

He walked down the hall and unlocked the door to his room. Walking in, he wondered how fast he could go with Rachel. Would she be interested in him? Or would she think she couldn't trust him? If Gunner had his choice, they'd be a couple and living together before Broken Hearts Brewing opened. He hated having to leave her and the kids last night. But if he had his way, he'd be the one taking care of all of them.

Growing up, he hadn't had a dad around. His mom had raised him and his two brothers. She was strong and did whatever it took to make sure they had what they needed. He could see the same kind of strength in Rachel. He was positive his mom would have loved her and the kids. His mom would have spoiled the kids because she'd always talked about grandkids. She'd passed before he, Brody, or Flick had given her any or even found their women.

A loud scream echoed from Brody's room. Gunner chuckled. He'd set the prank up for his brother two days ago. Brody hated roaches. He couldn't handle them. It didn't matter that Brody could deal with the cows and the horses. There was something about roaches that made him freak out when they were close to him.

Gunner had hooked up a little spring that, when Brody opened a cabinet, would release a little slingshot filled with fake rubbery cockroaches. And it sounded like his little prank had been very successful.

Brody needed to get his heart rate up anyway. Gunner was just being a good brother.

Banging on his bathroom door had Gunner double-checking he'd locked it as he got out of the shower and dried off.

"You won't know where and you won't know when, but I will get you back, you jerk," Brody yelled through the door.

"Oh, I'm so scared. What will I do?" Gunner called in a falsetto.

He grinned, slipping on his clothes and running a quick brush through his hair after brushing his teeth. He'd need to be on his guard because Brody would be gunning for payback, but Brody wouldn't be able to get one over on the master prankster.

He grabbed his cut, slipping it on over his T-shirt. He checked his watch—just enough time for a cinnamon roll before the ride. Yeah—life was good.

CHAPTER SIX

Rachel walked into Broken Hearts Brewing and marveled at the space. A furniture truck had pulled away as she parked her van. The wood floors gleamed. Two groupings of chairs and sofas created cozy spaces for people to relax. The shelves were all cleaned off and ready for merchandise.

Tables with chairs were set in the space, and the bar against the front window had tall chairs just waiting for people to enjoy the area. She could see all the interesting items she'd thought of for the shop on the shelves, just ready for people to enjoy.

"Hey, what do you think of the furniture? The women picked it out, but we can move it if you think stuff would look better somewhere else," Gunner said, coming out of the kitchen.

"I love it. I think it looks great where it is. I know we talked about an evening soft opening of family and friends. I think that will let us know if anything needs to be moved," Rachel said, grinning.

She probably looked like a fool, but she could barely contain the excitement of not only getting to showcase her crafts but also having a say in activities at the shop.

"I've been dying to find out what creations you've made. Did you bring them in that basket?" Gunner asked.

Rachel nodded, sitting down at the table. Gunner joined her, cocking his eyebrow.

"So, I had this idea about what we offered. I have these cats that I make that are super soft and cuddly. So let me introduce you to them and see what you think. This is Cina. Since the vibe of Broken Hearts Brewing is about recovering after a breakup or losing someone, I thought naming the cats would be cool. People could pick their cat for their recovery box. Cina's named for oxytocin, which is the chemical that, besides forming bonds between a mother and child, forms bonds between romantic partners," Rachel said quickly, handing the pink cat to Gunner.

He rubbed his fingers along the cat and then rubbed it against his neck.

"I'm just going to say your idea has blown me away. This is brilliant. They can come in for a drink and go home with something to cuddle with. Now, I know if you've thought about it this much, then you've got other ideas too. What are they?" Gunner asked, grinning at her.

Rachel breathed deep and let out all the worry she'd felt. Gunner loved her ideas. It was such a relief. Although she hadn't been able to crochet last night, she'd spent a couple hours this morning after she'd eaten to crochet the cats and write out her ideas.

"This one, I wanted your opinion on the name," she said, handing the black one to him.

"I was vacillating between Sera for serotonin, one of the feel-good chemicals, or Mina for dopamine. Dopamine influences your mood, among other things. Serotonin helps with multiple things but also helps with wound healing," Rachel said.

"I like both of them. Hmm, I really want to pick the right one. Maybe we could leave that one for now. If you don't have strong feelings, maybe we could ask Clara or Regina for help," Gunner suggested.

Rachel liked that idea because picking names was a big deal to her. She nodded and pulled out her next one.

"This yellow one is another one I was trying to decide," she said.

Gunner took the cat, petting it like it was a real cat. She giggled at his expression.

"It's very soothing. Did you have ideas?" he asked.

"Buttercup for *Buckle Up, Buttercup* is kind of sarcastic, like, hey, buckle up because it will be hard, but you'll get through it. On the other hand, I was considering Sunshine as a reminder that you'll get through this. It would be something people could send to those they thought might need to be cheered up," Rachel said.

Gunner chuckled. "Man, you're not making this easy. How are you thinking they'd know the names and what they're for?"

Rachel reached in her pack and pulled out little cards. "These are handmade, but I thought we could order some that talk about their names and offer encouragement," she said, handing them to Gunner.

He spent time reading them. Rachel was surprised that the silence didn't bother her. It was a comfortable silence that Rachel basked in. She loved her children, but sometimes, she needed the soothing quiet to have time to think. Maybe now that they were in a house and weren't on top of each other, she'd have more time where someone wasn't talking.

"I'm like you, I'm torn. I like both of them. Table that for a minute. Any more?" he asked.

She pulled out her deep purple one. "Purple is a symbol of royalty and being loyal. I was trying to think of a royal name. I thought of Queen or Queenie. I considered great queens like Wilhelmina or the classics like Catherine, Cleopatra, etc."

"Oh wow, the softness of this yarn is very soothing," Gunner said.

Rachel had been doing so well keeping business first in her mind, but Gunner's fingers sliding over the cat's fur had her mind going to his fingers sliding over her skin. Were his fingers a little rough from working in the kitchen, and how would that feel against her skin?

Whew! Was it getting hot in here?

She didn't understand what was happening. She didn't know Gunner. Sure, he'd helped last night, but anyone could show a nice side for a while—or sometimes years. Was it because it had been so long since she'd felt desire? Was she just latching onto the first male who treated her with respect and listened to her? Did she crave safety so much that she was desiring him because he would protect her and the kids?

She needed to not be so close to him, or she might forget her vow to make sure it was safe here before letting people in. If she let them in, then she'd have to face what had happened before they left. New friends wouldn't be fine with her keeping secrets. And she wasn't in a place to start a relationship.

She stood up and walked over to the bookcases.

"I was thinking here besides books, we could have mini bookshelves that they could buy. Next to the mini books of their favorite authors, we could have cute little things to go on the shelves too. What do you think about that?" Rachel asked.

Did he realize she'd stood up to get away from him because being close enough to smell his after-shave was giving her way too many ideas?

Gunner stood up and walked over by her.

Friggin' fudgesicles. She'd heard one of the kids say it yesterday. It definitely fit her mood right now. She swallowed because her mouth was dry and her heart was pounding. She felt out of control. If she let herself feel, would she break into a million little pieces?

This was a new start for both her and the kids. Her hormones needed to calm down. She needed to know she could trust Gunner or any of the other men before she dropped her panties. Was she really free to drop her panties for anyone? Her stomach soured at the thought of her situation.

How was she going to survive working with him every day?

Gunner stood beside Rachel, staring at the book-case because if he didn't, he'd be grabbing her by those cute-as-fuck jean overalls and kissing her, tasting her smiling lips that were so distracting.

He hoped he'd made the correct replies to her little crocheted cats. He thought they were cute, and he was positive they'd be popular. But staring at her sweet, smiling face while she described her thought processes had him wondering if she'd smile when he had her under him or over him. At this point, he didn't care; he just wanted her. His instant attraction was deepening as he got to know more about the woman who had knocked him on his ass.

It was making it hell on his self-control to go slow and give her time. Right now, if he could kick his own ass, he would because he wanted to say to hell with giving her time and taste her lips.

Banging on the front door saved him from having to decide if he was going to kiss her.

"Just a second," he said, walking to the front door and unlocking it. Phoebe, Blake, Deborah, and Benji stood outside.

"Can I help you?" he asked.

"I'm babysitting today. Blake and Phoebe saw you were in the shop and said they needed to talk with you about something," Deborah said.

"Well, come in. I think you all met Rachel yesterday. Let's sit down, and we can talk about whatever you wanted to talk with us about," Gunner said.

He pulled a couple extra chairs over so they could all sit together, waiting until the women sat before he did.

"We have a proposition for you," Blake said softly.

Gunner only hoped it was a legal one, because with these kids, he'd learned anything was possible. Their subscription service for swear words was genius.

"I think Rachel and I would like to hear it," Gunner said.

Blake nudged Phoebe.

"We want to be entrepreneurs cuz the only job girls usually get when they're young is babysitting. And we don't want to deal with babies. No offense, Deborah," Phoebe said.

Gunner bit his lip, glancing over at Rachel to see how she was handling the kids. Rachel seemed to be having the same issue he was, trying not to laugh. Gunner glanced back at the kids because it was so hard not to chuckle.

"None taken, Phoebe. I like kids and don't mind babysitting. If you don't, it's good you're thinking of other things," Deborah said.

"So what is your idea? An entrepreneur needs a concept or idea to get started," Rachel said.

"Blake and I like to take pictures. We thought we could make them into cards people could buy," Phoebe said, motioning to Blake.

Blake placed her backpack on the table and took out two cards.

Gunner examined the cards. The front was a picture of a monarch butterfly on a bush. The inside was blank. The back had *Designs by Phoebe and Blake*. He had to admit he was impressed.

"Did you get these printed?" Gunner asked.

"Yep. Mom helped me order a sample set. She said if you sold them that we could do a consignment model or wholesale model. But then Joey started crying and she had to take care of him. She didn't explain," Phoebe said, rolling her eyes.

Gunner bit his lip. These kids always made him smile and sometimes laugh, but he didn't want to hurt their feelings by laughing. He was impressed with their idea.

"Consignment model would be that we would put your cards for sale in the shop. When they sell, you would get a set portion of the sale. Let's say sixty percent for you and forty percent for the shop. Money would be paid out at the end of the month. A wholesale model means that you would sell it at a cheaper price to us, but we would pay you upfront when the cards come into the store. Let's say with that, we'd pay you forty percent of the total amount we'd sell them for. Usually with consignment, if they don't sell, they would be returned to you. With wholesale, if they don't sell, we, the business, absorb the loss," Rachel explained.

"Me and Blake might need to discuss this," Phoebe said.

"Well, how about you and Blake discuss it for a minute while I chat with Rachel regarding it?" Gunner said.

At Phoebe's nod, he and Rachel walked over to the counter.

Rachel was almost bouncing; she was so excited. "Oh my gosh. What a fantastic idea. Do you love it as much as I do? And we could let some of the other kids come up with ideas too? There are a couple of easy crochet patterns the kids could learn if they want."

Gunner grinned because they were on the same wavelength. "I agree. It would be good for the kids and their families. Besides helping the kids, it would guarantee us that customers would come to see the kids' stuff. It would definitely be a win-win."

"I love the idea of helping kids realize that their ideas and dreams are achievable," Rachel said.

Gunner had taken the idea of the shop and run with it because he loved the idea of being his own boss. The extra bonus of feeding people and making them happy had been such a win. But sharing the joy of this with the younger generation of Bluff Creek had him knowing he was doing the right thing.

Sitting back down, he nodded at Rachel to take the lead.

"We would love to stock your cards. They are beautiful, and we both love that you took the initiative to do this. We're five weeks before opening, and Gunner and I haven't made up any contracts yet. I've only been in town a little bit. Would it be okay if we set up a meeting for next week, and we could have contracts available then?" Rachel asked.

Phoebe and Blake both nodded, their eyes almost as wide as the grins on their faces.

"We're really excited you brought this idea to us, and we can't wait to work with you both," Gunner said.

"Hey, I don't want to babysit people either, but I can't take pictures. If I figure out something to sell, can I come to the meeting too?" Benji asked.

"Of course," Gunner said. He stared at Benji.

"You've brought up a good point. Let Rachel and me talk about it. We might need to set up a certain time that we can have proposals brought up next week."

"Thank you!" Phoebe, Blake, and Benji yelled. The kids got up and started discussing what they could do as they walked out the door.

"Thank you," Deborah said, following the kids out.

Rachel hopped up and stared at the bookshelves, spinning around to look at the room.

"Maybe we could add a table here with items made by kids to highlight them. Oh, I have so many ideas," Rachel said.

"I think it sounds great, but how about I show you the rest of the shop and then we can make a list?" Gunner said.

Listening to Rachel agree and then immediately start talking about something else had Gunner knowing, yep, she was going to be his, but he needed a better plan than he had. He wondered if Clara might have any suggestions.

CHAPTER SEVEN

Gunner chuckled as he walked toward Clara's house. It was a Saturday night, and he was going to Clara's to get her take on Rachel.

Regina and Baron, along with Rascal and Meg, were having a movie night with the kids. He'd heard Beth ask Rachel to come over to her house for a movie night with some of the women.

Last night, after he'd gone to bed, and when he woke up this morning, he couldn't get what Marcus had told him about his dad and Chelle calling her dad a bad daddy out of his head. He and Rachel had gone over items at the store, but it kept rolling around in his head—what Marcus had said was something Rachel needed to know if she didn't.

His gut was telling him that he needed to talk about this with her, but he didn't want to cause her more pain. He also had no idea of the status of Rachel's relationship with her husband.

Earlier, Clara had told him she'd be in the kitchen and to just walk in. So he did.

"I'm here, Clara," Gunner called.

"In the kitchen."

Gunner paused in the doorway, then walked over to the sink to wash his hands. Clara had bowls and cookie sheets on the table in her kitchen.

"You said you needed to talk, and I always talk better when I'm also working on something," she said.

"What are we making?" he asked.

"Well, I know they may not be up to the intricate items you make, but I wanted peanut butter blossoms. I've also never made spritz cookies but always wanted to try. I have a brand new spritz machine, and I bought ingredients for a couple different recipes. What do you think?" Clara asked, grinning at him.

Standing in her kitchen with the supplies around made him miss his mom. Sharing this time with Clara would be special too. Not the same but different.

"I think we need to get to work. What first?" he asked, sitting down.

"I mixed up the dough for the peanut butter blossoms, so let's start on those," Clara said, pushing a bowl toward him.

"Now, what do we need to talk about?" Clara asked, rolling the dough into a ball, then rolling it in sugar before placing it on the cookie sheet.

"Marcus shared something. I feel like I need to tell Rachel, but I don't want to walk into the situation blind. I don't want you to break a confidence, but are she and her husband still married?" Gunner asked.

"It's not breaking a confidence. Rachel gave me all the information, and it's been shared with Scoop and Sarah for them to do some research. I believe if Rachel hadn't shown up early, Scoop was supposed to share the situation with all of you in council tomorrow," Clara said, rolling another ball and dipping it in sugar.

"Well, am I going to need to pull it out of you?" Gunner grumbled.

Clara smiled, and if he wasn't mistaken, he recognized her mischievous look.

"No, but what are your intentions toward Rachel and the kids?" Clara asked.

Gunner rolled a couple cookies, dipping them in sugar, stopping to stare at Clara.

"She's mine. They all are, but I don't want to do anything to remind her of 'bad daddy'," Gunner said.

Clara nodded. "Good answer. Over a year ago, I met Rachel online in a craft forum. We started chatting over patterns and then drifted into family. She said she was married but things had changed. She was going to go see a divorce lawyer. Before she could, he left, taking anything of value in the house that could be sold and cleaned out one of their bank accounts. Rachel had already moved some money and her craft money to another account. She wasn't destitute. She suspected he'd started gambling and she had found drug paraphernalia. He was nowhere to be found afterward. The police department said she couldn't file anything against him because he had rights to everything in the house. He'd also taken from a joint bank account. Her lawyer must have been a loser because he basically told her not to worry about it."

"What a jerk," Gunner said.

"I agree. Fast forward to the Saturday after Thanksgiving when I went to the craft fair, and I talked with her about the job. She decided to come but she wanted to wait until after Christmas. They'd already decorated, and she had presents wrapped under the tree. The kids wanted to finish this semester with their school friends and both kids had parts in the school play," Clara said, getting up to put one of the trays in the oven.

She poured both of them drinks and sat back down. Taking a drink, she swallowed, then stared at Gunner.

"Every time I think about this, I want to go find him and pop his head right off his neck," Clara grumbled.

Gunner reached over and patted Clara's hand.

"I'll tell you, but you can't change how you treat her. She's strong, and she doesn't want to be seen as a victim. Do you promise?" Clara asked.

"I do," he said. Clara patted his hand back.

"They had a fantastic Christmas together. The kids loved the toys that Rachel was able to buy them. Rachel had an after-Christmas craft fair. She and the kids drove to it and spent the weekend there. When they returned home, one of her neighbors came running over. Her missing husband had returned and had a yard sale while they were gone. He'd sold almost everything. The neighbor had tried to call Rachel and tell her but was unable to reach her. The only things that were left were the items that Rachel had in her van and the small amount of stuff that she'd started moving to a storage building as she packed. She also couldn't go in the house because he had told the landlord that they were moving and needed the deposit back. The landlord had changed the locks, and suddenly Rachel and the kids were homeless," Clara said.

A wave of anger washed over Gunner. If he had her husband in front of him, he wasn't sure he wouldn't beat the man until he couldn't walk.

"How could he do that if the lease was in both their names?" Gunner asked.

"Exactly what Rachel wondered. She'd noticed the landlord and her husband being very chummy a couple of times. She has no proof, but she wonders if the landlord got a cut from what her husband sold," Clara said.

Gunner got back to rolling the cookies because he needed something to do with his hands. How was he going to show Rachel and the kids that they could trust him?

"Where'd she live?" he asked.

"Kansas City," Clara said.

"Well, that I can work with," Gunner said.

Clara chuckled and got up to pull a cookie sheet out of the oven and add the chocolate kisses.

"Hmm, could you be thinking of contacting the Saint's Outlaws MC possibly?" Clara asked.

"Oh, you can count on it," Gunner said.

He and Clara chatted as they finished the peanut butter cookies and then started on the spritz cookies. When they were finished, Gunner washed the cookie sheets and bowls after sending Clara to go sit in front of the television. She had a show she liked to watch.

Once the dishes were done and the counters were clean, Gunner walked into the front room, leaning over to kiss Clara's cheek.

"Thank you for a fun evening. I'm going to make sure that Rachel, Chelle, and Marcus never want for anything," Gunner vowed.

Clara patted his face. "I know you will, Gunner, because you are a good man. You're exactly the man they need. Grab some of those cookies to take with you and share them with the boys in the clubhouse," she said.

He nodded, grabbed one of the containers and walked out the door. Oh, he'd definitely share with the boys in the clubhouse. He'd also share that she called them boys just because he enjoyed teasing his friends.

Rachel took a sip of her soda. It had been a long day, and Rachel was ready to head to bed. Between not sleeping well because her head hurt and then meeting Gunner, she'd been going all day long.

Her new friends had wanted to welcome her, and despite being tired, she couldn't say no. She'd tried to remember something about each of the women she'd met tonight. The Franks sisters were easy because Clara had talked about them so much. Remi, the oldest who ran the bail bonds, and Sarah, who was the tech person, had both given her hugs as soon as she walked in.

Winnie, who ran the bail bonds gym, and Jesse, who ran the garage, were in the kitchen fixing drinks for everyone. Beth had taken her around to introduce her to the women, but she'd told them that they might need to tell her their names again.

"Hey, Stella, how are you doing without Rose or Tasha here?" Remi asked.

"It's been different," Stella said, taking a sip of her drink.

"Oh yeah, it's been different. I've heard that truck pulling in as you get dropped off some mornings. It always leaves so fast that I don't have time to get up and to the window to see who it is," Hope said, chuckling.

Rachel was sure Hope was married to Locks and was Faith's sister. Her son Benji had asked Marcus to play.

Stella blushed, and Rachel had to join in the laughter with the other women.

"What are you—the neighborhood watch?" Stella sputtered.

"Oh, way to try to deflect. Do we know the mystery man?" Faith asked.

Stella rolled her eyes. "It's new, and I'm not sure I'm ready to share yet."

"Fair enough. We have new blood to interrogate. I mean, get to know," Frankie said.

Rachel grinned. Frankie had introduced herself and marveled over what she called Rachel's virgin skin. She, Harry, and Emerson worked at Bluff Creek Ink and had offered her a free tattoo if they got to be the first.

"Come sit by me. I'll protect you," Beth said.

Rachel settled by Beth.

"Since I'm married to War, I know about your situation. I want to tell you that this is a safe place, and we'll be better able to take care of you if you share. But if you'd prefer not to talk about it, then I can let people know later. Your safety and that of your kids is a priority for us," Remi said.

"You all seem so put together that I'll feel like a failure if you know," Rachel said.

Chuckles filled the room. Rachel didn't feel like they were mean but almost as if she wasn't in on the joke.

"Well, let me share my story. I had a really good friend in the Army who I knew could be more, but I was eventually getting out. He was planning on being in for life, and I couldn't see being the one who only saw him maybe once a year. Fast forward a few years, and a man who terrorized me in the military was getting out. Bluff Creek offered me a safe space. Cruise, the man I'd fallen for, was here. He and the Franks sisters helped me get justice. And I'm Willa. I know it's a lot of names to remember," Willa said.

"What we're saying is, we won't judge you. Everyone has a story with valleys and mountains. What matters is that we keep moving forward to a better place," Sarah said.

"Yeah, Remi's love story includes pranks with her high school enemy and a roadside shootout," Winnie said.

"Two shootouts if you're being accurate. Don't forget the one in the hotel," Remi said.

"I'm sure you can tell Remi is the oldest and knows everything," Winnie muttered.

Rachel smiled at the teasing. She hoped her kids would have this tight bond when they grew up.

"I was the kid in high school who was a free spirit. I could get B's and some A's without studying.

Why would I worry about studying when I could be reading and crafting instead?

"My senior year of high school, right before graduation, I slept with my boyfriend. We had grand dreams of him being a long-haul trucker and me being an artist. My parents found out I wasn't going to college and wanted to get married. Their supportive answer was to kick me out," Rachel said.

"Oh, I'm sorry," Beth said, patting Rachel's arm. The comfort of that touch grounded Rachel. Sharing her story could possibly be healing.

"When we started dating, it was that thrill of young love. We stayed together, and then I got pregnant with Marcus, followed quickly by Chelle. I adore my kids. Meanwhile, I figured out which of my crafts sold and started making money at craft fairs. When he'd come home, he'd want me to wait on him because he was the man of the house. Now, I have no problem doing something for my spouse if it's reciprocal. Sometimes I get things for him and sometimes he gets things for me. This is not the 1950s, where women couldn't have their own checking accounts and men were supposed to be in charge of everything," Rachel said.

"Preach, Sister," Emerson yelled, her hand in the air.

"You're such a dork," Harry said, giggling.

"Listen, little sis, I have so many stories I can tell if you start bugging me," Emerson said.

"Ladies, let's get back to Rachel's story. I am invested," Sarah said.

"A little over a year ago, Maynard came home and wasn't acting the same. I'd noticed some erratic behavior before, so I had started a separate account with my crafting money. My small-time crafting was turning into a business. I was starting to save for a divorce attorney. Before I could, he cleaned out the joint account we had and took items to sell. I suspected he was either drinking or using drugs. I also wondered if he was gambling because of how much money he was removing from our accounts each week.

"He was gone and I thought we were good. Fast forward to December. I hadn't seen or heard from him for a year. The kids and I had a great Christmas, and then we left for my after-Christmas craft fair. I'd already started packing some items because Clara had offered me the job here. We returned home to find that he'd shown up and cleared us out. He also told the landlord we were moving and that he needed the deposit back. Suddenly, we had no home, and half the kids' stuff was gone.

"I despise the father of my children, and I'm so freaking angry," Rachel said, sniffing and wiping the tears she hadn't realized were running down her face.

"First off, I am so sorry you've gone through that. Second, I've only seen you smiling since you got here. I'm impressed with how you're dealing with it," Frankie said.

Rachel forced a smile. "My mom always saw the worst in all situations. If the meal was half off, she always thought it should have been sixty percent off. I vowed when I had kids that I would always look for the bright side of things. I wouldn't subject my kids to the constant negativity I grew up with. I've found a new home, a new job, and new friends to help me keep my kids safe. I'd say—I'm doing well."

"Anger isn't a bad thing. Sometimes, anger fuels us to do the things that need to be done. I want to share something with you that normally we only do on special occasions, but everyone in the room is a part of it. My sisters and I started an organization after our mom passed to honor her and also help those in need. Kathryn's Wings has safe houses and helpers all over Texas, Oklahoma, Kansas, Nebraska, and South Dakota. We've recently added Colorado. Women, children, and even men who've been abused or need help out of a situation can have a new start.

"You've gone through a situation that you have every right to be mad about and none of it is your fault. Sometimes a loved one chooses a different path that doesn't put their family first. Since I don't know what exactly caused your husband to do what he did, I can't say what his motivation was. What I can say is we will keep you and your kids safe. If you could choose to resolve the situation any way you could, what would be your choice?" Remi asked.

Rachel thought through how, in the year before he left, that he'd completely ignored both kids. She remembered noticing in that last month that Chelle and Marcus had stopped running to him when he walked in the door. She hadn't seen any hugs or affection between them, and that's when she decided it was time to part ways with him.

"I would want a divorce and full custody of both my children. I don't want the money back if it means he's in our lives. I don't trust him with the kids," Rachel said.

Remi nodded. "We can work with that. I know tomorrow is Sunday and we all have lunch together. War has called council for directly after lunch. I'll chat with him tonight and let him know your wishes," Remi said.

"Now, let's chat about fun things. Rachel, we have a book club, but with the opening of Broken Hearts Brewing, we wondered what all you were thinking of offering since you'll be stocking books too," Winnie asked.

Rachel grinned at the light in Winnie's eyes. She loved being around other readers and couldn't wait to discover what types of books they enjoyed.

She took a deep breath and realized she could share her dreams with this group. The support tonight meant the world to her.

CHAPTER EIGHT

Rachel giggled at the antics on the couch. They'd just finished a wonderful lunch. Rachel had offered to take a turn cleaning up, but Regina had informed her that her first Sunday in Bluff Creek didn't include dishes. Next week, Rachel could join the rotation.

Stone and Gunner were allowing Phoebe, Blake, and Chelle to paint their nails while they discussed the girls' obsession with unicorns. Rachel was thrilled that Chelle had found two other girls as in love with unicorns as she was.

Chelle had Rachel read to her anything Rachel could find on the topic. When Rachel had heard that Phoebe was as obsessed with them as Chelle, Rachel had been thrilled. Stone had informed the group he was helping Phoebe illustrate the story she was writing about a unicorn.

"Gunner, do you think unicorns are special too?" Chelle asked.

Rachel adored that Chelle felt comfortable enough to share her favorite thing with Gunner.

"I do. Over the ages, they've been seen as strong, loyal, and chivalrous," he said.

"What's chival-tus?" she asked, sticking her tongue between her teeth.

"Chiv- ul -rus," he sounded out for her. Chelle repeating it back to him was the cutest thing.

"It means being gallant, which is another word for courteous, especially toward women. It can also mean being brave in battle," Gunner said.

"I like that," Phoebe replied.

"Me too," Chelle said.

"When I get older, I want a tattoo of a unicorn on my arm," Blake said.

"Why the heck would you want one of that stupid make-believe animal on your arm?" Finn, who had just walked back into the room, muttered.

"You take that back! Unicorns are chiv- ul… cool!" Chelle yelled, tears starting to form in her eyes.

Stone stood up, lifting Chelle over to put her on Gunner's lap. "You stay right here, and I'll take care of the naysayer disparaging unicorns," Stone said, bopping her on the nose, then walking toward Finn.

"Well, you stepped in it this time," Stone said, shaking his head.

"War, we have something we need to discuss about Finn disparaging unicorns to Chelle, Blake, and Phoebe," Stone yelled, the words echoing in the room as everyone quieted.

"It's time for council anyway. We can discuss it first," War said.

"Rachel, we thought we would discuss your situation in council. You may come in to listen if you like, or if you'd prefer not to go through it, then we can just jot down any questions we have," War said.

"I think I'll wait for your questions," Rachel said.

Gunner walked over, carrying Chelle. "If you're good, I'll go to council. I'd love to take a walk with you afterward. Bear and Winnie are having afternoon fun for the kids until five p.m."

"Sounds good," she said, starting to take Chelle from his arms, but Chelle shook her head.

"I'm fine. I just like when Gunner carries me," Chelle said, hugging Rachel quickly before running back over by Blake and Phoebe.

Gunner sat down by Stone at the table, waiting for War to call them to order. Yeah, so he was being a little bit of a dick, glaring at Finn, but there was no need for Finn's outburst when the kids were there.

Gunner didn't give a flying fuck if Finn said crap about unicorns. What he did care about was an adult putting down a child's ideas. Children needed to be able to dream without constraints.

Finn's thoughtless, sarcastic words sent a message that Gunner didn't agree with.

War banged a gavel on the table. "Order!"

Everyone quieted. Gunner wondered which issue War would have them dealing with first.

"Let's get this out of the way. Finn, although you and Ben are allowed in meetings, you're still considered Prospects in a probationary period. I thought what you did was rude. If Amelia was that age and you said that to her, I probably would have wanted to string you up like a piñata and beat some sense into you. Now, my wife and her sisters, however, are devious," War said, pausing for the laughter to die down.

"They suggested a punishment that I think fits the crime perfectly. They suggested that for the next three months, everywhere you go, you will need to take and wear a pink unicorn backpack. And since your behavior was what the Franks sisters consider juvenile, they'd like the brotherhood to consider that, in addition to the unicorn backpack, you be required to ride the small electric Razor motorbike instead of your motorcycle," War said.

Gunner slapped the table, his shoulders shaking. Glancing at Stone beside him, Gunner saw the biggest grin on Stone's face.

"Yes, yes, yes," Stone yelled in reply.

War let them laugh and tease Finn for a little bit before quieting everyone down.

"Let's vote on the issues separately. All in favor of making Finn wear the unicorn backpack whenever he leaves the clubhouse for the next three months—no exceptions. All in favor?" War asked.

Gunner bit his lip at the show of hands. It was unanimous.

"Well, guess we don't need to ask if there are any nays. Second point, all in favor of Finn being required to ride the small electric Razor motorbike instead of his motorcycle for the same three months. All in favor?" War asked.

In no time, Finn had his penalties, and War had sent Finn and Ben out of the room.

"I have no problem with our prospects knowing the next bit of information, but after today, I thought it couldn't hurt to remind them of their status. Now, Scoop, can you update us?" War said.

Scoop clicked a couple buttons and a picture appeared on the screen on the wall.

"Meet Maynard, jerk extraordinaire, who emptied his and Rachel's main checking and savings accounts a year ago while also stealing things from the house to sell. He then disappeared for a year. Rachel was getting ready to file for divorce. Her lawyer wasn't willing to do anything when he left," Scoop said.

"Where did she live?" Roam asked.

"Kansas City. I plan on contacting Adley to see if she can help and maybe make a call to their flower shop for a *Get Well* delivery. I'd rather take care of the guy myself, but I will not have those kids see me being violent. They need to understand we're a safe place," Gunner said.

Every time he thought of Rachel just being ignored by the people meant to help her, he couldn't contain the anger.

"Good idea. Remi is already adding his name to their list of people to find. Since he isn't technically a bounty, Remi and I are offering one to any of the bail bonds employees who find him," War said.

"I'm happy to toss some cash that way too if you need to sweeten the bounty. I have plenty of cash and would be happy to have some of it go to getting this guy out of Rachel's and the kids' lives," Stone said.

"Thanks," Gunner muttered. Stone's hand giving a reassuring squeeze to his shoulder helped him stay calm.

"Stone, if you keep chatting like this, then who are all the women going to gossip about?" Scoop teased.

"Oh, they'll be chatting about brooding Brody," Cannon replied.

"Who calls me brooding?" Brody said.

Gunner bit his lip to keep from grinning at Brody's irritated tone. He had to admit Brody had been brooding some. Gunner wondered if it had to do with him starting to work with Savi on the K9 training and rescue.

"Oh, my wife, her sisters, and half the women on the compound," Cannon said.

"Could we possibly get back on track?" War said, pinching the bridge of his nose.

Oh, Gunner would be doing the same thing if he was in charge of keeping all the brothers on track.

"Gunner, we'll wait to hear from you about reaching out to the Saint's Outlaws and also to see if any of the bail bonds employees find anything. Until then, keep an eye out for Rachel's husband," War said.

"Estranged husband," Gunner growled.

Gunner didn't appreciate the glee in War's voice when he replied *noted*. So sue him if he wanted to differentiate. As far as Gunner was concerned, Rachel was a free agent because her husband had abandoned her, Marcus, and Chelle. The divorce papers would just be a technicality.

"We're done until next week," War said, dismissing them.

Gunner walked out, grabbing his phone from the basket. He wanted to see if Rachel would take a walk with him.

Thankfully, when he walked into the main room, Rachel was sitting on the couch talking with Clara. He walked over, wondering what he'd done to have her sweep into his life because she was a gift. Now he had to convince her that they were meant to be.

"Rachel, would you like to go on a walk with me?" Gunner asked.

CHAPTER NINE

Rachel stared at Gunner's face, examining each inch for a hint of his intentions for the walk. All she found was his smile.

"Oh, go on. We can chat crochet patterns later," Clara said.

"I'd like that," Rachel replied.

She took his outstretched hand, letting him lead her out the door. She was glad she had a long-sleeved shirt with a flannel on under her jean overalls. The sunny January day was warm for this time of year, but there was still a little nip in the air.

"I thought we could get to know each other and also maybe bounce ideas about the shop—basically whatever you wanted," Gunner said.

She glanced toward him, then turned to the scenery. Where to start? Was he going to ask questions?

"It's been a whirlwind since you arrived. I know, at least from Scoop's point of view, what you went through. I thought it might be good if you knew more about me," he said.

He paused and almost seemed as if he was waiting for her agreement. She nodded because he seemed so hesitant, which wasn't how she'd viewed him before today.

"I grew up with Brody and Flick. I was the prankster in school because Brody's the oldest, and let's just say—that stick has been lodged up his ass a long time."

She couldn't help giggling. Brody did seem to be wound a little tight.

"Mom was a single mom. I don't really remember when Dad left. I always loved working in the kitchen with her—baking and cooking. I loved making recipes and seeing the joy on people's faces when they enjoyed the food. I served in the military and then got out to pursue culinary arts.

"I jumped at the chance of running Broken Hearts Brewing when Beth brought it up as an idea when they were on an undercover assignment. It was as if she knew exactly what job I wanted. Beth and Flick got married in July, and Brody got out of the service after being injured. Beth had us both move in with them after their wedding. She wanted us to have a family again," Gunner said.

"How was that?" Rachel asked.

Gunner grinned and shook his head. "Well, my sister-in-law definitely let us know if we were screwing up. I will never leave a toilet seat up again," he said.

Rachel loved hearing about their family. She wanted her kids to experience a happy family where everyone loved each other.

"Anything you want to share?" he asked.

She thought about everything she'd been through. Besides the women last night, she hadn't been asked to share. Gunner asking her gave her the nudge she needed to open up.

"So you know that my husband cleaned out the accounts, stole some stuff, and left a year ago. I have so many regrets," she said.

"About losing him?" Gunner asked.

"Oh, heck no. Regrets that I didn't get him served earlier. Now I'm in this kind of limbo. I don't feel married because we are done. But it's dragging out. I keep a happy face because I never want to be my negative mother, but there's this big issue standing in the way of me moving on," Rachel said.

"I don't think talking about our feelings is negative. Sometimes we need to vent," Gunner said.

"Oh, I agree. I don't want my kids to in any way see that I'm sad and possibly come to the wrong conclusion that it was caused by them. Does that make sense?" she asked.

Gunner paused by a barbed-wire fence. A dirt track and large tree were on the other side of the pasture.

"It does. You want to protect your kids. That's exactly what a good mom does. I've debated how to say this to you, but I wouldn't feel comfortable not telling you something. You may already know but if you don't, I'd never forgive myself for not telling you," Gunner said.

Rachel turned toward Gunner. His serious face told her all she needed to know. What he had to tell her was not going to be anything that made her happy, but he said she needed to know.

"Okay, I'm ready," Rachel said. Whatever he said, she could deal with. She and the kids were safe here.

"When you hit your head and we had to call Stella and Flick, Marcus was upset. Once he calmed down, he said he had a secret. Marcus said that bad daddy had threatened him that if Marcus told you what he saw, bad daddy would kill you and Chelle," Gunner's words hit her.

A wave of cold washed over her. He did what? And Marcus was too scared to say anything?

How could she have missed how far her husband had sunk? What type of mom was she? She'd tried to be everything they needed but she could only do so much. Doing it all made her so tired.

She'd missed this huge thing, and she really wished Maynard was right in front of her this minute.

"Rachel, are you okay? Stone and I assured Marcus you all were safe," Gunner said softly.

"I'm not okay. I want to chase him down and beat him until he can't threaten my kids ever again. I just am so angry I feel like I'm going to explode," Rachel said through gritted teeth.

Her fingers itched to grasp Maynard's neck and teach him to never, ever hurt her children again.

"We need to test out the smash room at Broken Hearts. How about I take you there and you can break some stuff?" Gunner asked.

Rachel nodded. Yes, she needed to break something, or she'd never get all this anger out. She let Gunner lead her back toward the clubhouse. It was a blur as Gunner got her a heavy jacket and helmet for his bike. She wrapped her hands around his waist as he took them back into town. He'd even taken care of letting Bear and Winnie know where they were going.

Why had she not realized something else was going on before her little man was threatened by someone? Someone who should be doing every-thing they could to keep him safe. How did she repair what her husband had broken? Was it even possible?

How did she get past this? She'd already felt bad about not seeking a divorce earlier. How could she ever forgive herself?

Gunner's voice asking her if she was ready to get off his bike pulled her from her downward spiral. He unlocked the door and led her in.

He'd mentioned the room, but he hadn't gone over procedures. He talked her through taking off the jacket and sliding the large coveralls over her clothes. She tucked her shoes in the cubby against the wall, slipping on the ones provided along with the shoe covers. Her ensemble was completed by sliding the hood over her hair and putting on the protective glasses and gloves.

Once Gunner had helped her, he quick-ly slipped on his protective gear. Leading her through the door, he grabbed an old large televi-sion, setting it on the cement table in the middle of the room. He stared at her for a minute before going to a pile of items and picking out a large computer console. Setting it beside the TV, he went back over to the pile. He placed a large metal plant holder that had a hole rusted in the bottom.

He led her over to the wall where she could pick out what tools she wanted. She wanted to destroy stuff, but she wasn't a big girl. She didn't lift weights. She picked out a big mallet and swung it back and forth. Not too heavy for her. She grabbed a crowbar and walked over to the tables and turned back toward Gunner. He gave her a thumbs-up and pressed the buttons on the wall, turning the music on.

She stared at the items for a minute, trying to decide where to start. She breathed deeply and just let out all the rage she felt for the man she'd married and entrusted with their children.

The actions became a blur as she destroyed the ones on the table. Once the items were decimated, Gunner would make sure she wasn't swinging again and would replace them.

She lost track of the number of times he replaced the items. Finally, after she'd expended all the anger, she let go of the crowbar. The clang as it hit the floor was loud, even over the music. She dropped to the floor and let the tears she'd been holding back come.

Each time he'd broken her trust or her kids had to do without as she rebuilt their life, she'd pushed aside her feelings to just make it through. Gunner wrapped his arms around her and let her cry against him. He didn't try to tell her it would be better or that it wasn't her fault. He held her while she cried and let all those emotions out.

Rachel wasn't a pretty crier, and when she went to wipe her nose with her sleeve, Gunner stopped her.

"We're covered in glass. A little snot isn't going to bother me. Get the tears out, and then we'll get cleaned up," he said.

She turned to stare at him through her protective glasses that had fogged during her crying. No one had ever cared for her when she cried. Gunner was protective and was more worried about her hurting herself than about the snot running down her face.

"Why?" she asked.

"Why what?" he replied.

"Why are you helping me?" she asked.

He smiled, his teeth white against his tan skin and his beard.

"Friggin' fudgesicles," Gunner grunted, turning his head to stare at the ceiling. He turned back to her, shaking his head and smiling at her.

"I know you're probably not ready to hear this, but I can't start this by lying to you. When you opened that van door and I caught a glimpse of you, something happened. It was like that part of my life that was missing was there in front of me. And then, when I saw the kids, I was worried you were married and in love with someone else. My heart started to beat again when I realized you could be mine, and this is, like, the worst time to bring it up. But you mean too much to me to start us off with a lie," Gunner said.

What exactly was he saying? He wanted to have sex, or he wanted more? She wasn't sure, but the emotions swirling through her had her feeling adrift.

"Hey, I see your eyes looking at me with disbelief. You don't need to respond to anything I said. We're still co-workers and, I hope, friends. I can wait until you're ready for something more, but for now, I need you to know that I will do whatever it takes to ensure your safety and that of your children," Gunner said.

Rachel let him help her up and then out of the room, where they changed out of the protective clothing, putting it in a barrel to be cleaned later. Gunner flipped the light off. As she followed him out, she tugged his hand. She couldn't just say nothing. It was rude, and even though she was falling apart, she couldn't do that to him.

"I heard what you said. I appreciate you sharing that with me and not lying to me. It means the world to me. In the last four days, I've packed up my life, moved to a new place, and the kids start school tomorrow. I'm just not ready to respond because I feel like if I have to deal with one more thing, I'll break into a million pieces. I just need to get through a couple things and hold everything together," Rachel said.

Gunner nodded, and she had to wonder if he thought she was crazy and was rethinking what he'd said. The woman you profess to be attracted to admits that she might be a little crazy and heading toward a nervous breakdown.

Gunner grasped one of the straps of her overalls, tugging her closer until he leaned down far enough for their foreheads to touch. This close, she could smell his scent that she'd come to associate with safety. Just a little closer and his beard would brush her face.

"Take all the time you need. Whenever you feel like you're breaking into pieces, come find me. I'll always help hold you together," he said softly.

Rachel closed her eyes, slid her arms around his waist, and relaxed to breathe him in. He was a biker, a chef, and someone she trusted. Less than three days in Bluff Creek, and Gunner had broken through her walls. In his arms, she knew she could be herself. She wasn't sure how long they stood there, him holding her.

"You ready to go back?" Gunner asked.

She nodded and slid on the jacket, waiting while he helped fasten her helmet. She had a lot to think about, but one thing she was sure of was that she'd made a good decision coming to Bluff Creek.

CHAPTER TEN

Gunner ran up the steps to Rachel's house and knocked on the door. He was hoping no one saw him with the stupid grin on his face. He'd offered to drive Rachel and the kids to the first day of school, and she'd said yes.

Afterward, they were sitting down to plan for each week until the opening. Gunner had already been excited for Broken Hearts, but having a partner to work with, whom he absolutely adored, changed everything.

Marcus opened the door, hugging Gunner as soon as he came in.

"Are you ready for your first day of school here?"

Marcus nodded. "Yep, Mom found out last night that I get to be in the same class as Benji."

Gunner held his hand out for Marcus to high-five. "So you already have a friend in class. Where's your mom?"

Marcus pointed toward the bathroom.

"Okay, is Chelle ready?" Gunner asked.

"She's in her room," Marcus said, walking away to get his backpack.

Gunner walked into Chelle's room. She was sitting on her bed, dressed in a cute pair of jean overalls with a polka dot shirt underneath. Rachel had pulled her hair into a ponytail. Her backpack was on the bed.

"Are you ready for school?" Gunner asked.

Chelle shook her head.

Gunner knelt down. "What's up, buttercup?"

She giggled, then went back to frowning.

"Share the deets, Pete."

She giggled again, then frowned.

"Explain the problem... umm, I can't rhyme with problem. So what's the scoop, little boop?" Gunner asked.

Chelle hopped off the bed and grabbed Gunner's hand.

"What if no one likes me?" she asked.

"Aww, first days are so hard. Can I tell you a secret?" Gunner asked, turning to peek over his shoulder.

Chelle nodded, her eyes widening. Gunner leaned close.

"Almost everybody in school is worried people won't like them. Sometimes they just hide it better," Gunner whispered close to her ear.

Chelle scrunched her eyebrows. He worked not to chuckle at her face, which looked exactly like Rachel's sometimes.

"Promise?" she asked.

"I promise. Now, just say hi to everyone, and I want you to remember this: sometimes people may not talk much or may seem like they are ignoring you. But it could be because they are shy. So show them your pretty smile and meet some new people today. Now, do you want me to hold your hand?" he asked.

Chelle nodded and took his hand again. He grabbed her backpack. When they got out into the front room, Rachel was waiting with Marcus. He couldn't tell what was going on, but she seemed a little off.

They hustled the kids out to the SUV and headed toward the school. Marcus and Chelle asked questions about the town and the school. Gunner could answer some but not all. He might need to chat with Regina about the town. He didn't like not knowing the answer to the kids' questions.

In no time, they'd dropped the kids off at their classrooms, and he and Rachel headed to Broken Hearts Brewing. Rachel was quiet and the music wasn't on. Which was why, when she pressed a hand against her stomach and groaned quietly, he heard it.

"Okay, tell me what's going on. Are you okay?" he asked.

Oh dear God, he didn't ask her about her groan. She felt like total and complete dog crap. She took something for the pain and was just waiting for it to kick in.

Today was worse than some times, but still, it's not something she wanted to share with the man who said he liked her yesterday.

"Rachel, if you don't feel well, everything can wait. I want you to feel okay," Gunner said.

She didn't answer right away because she wasn't used to talking about this with anyone. Her mom had never discussed this with her, and after marriage, Maynard had shuddered whenever she brought it up.

Gunner made the turn onto the corner where Broken Hearts Brewing was and drove past.

"Hey, you missed stopping," Rachel said.

Gunner glanced over at her but kept driving away, back toward the compound.

"Something is obviously wrong, and you don't feel well. I'm taking you back to the house," he said.

Rachel hung her head. Fudge! She was going to have to tell him what was going on. It was just so embarrassing.

"I have cramps. They started this morning. They usually go away the second day," she muttered, her face warming. Was she really blushing like a teenager?

"Oh, well, why didn't you say so? Do you have a heating pad? What about medicine?" Gunner asked.

Rachel turned to stare at Gunner's profile. He'd just acted like it wasn't a big deal.

"Umm, I think my heating pad is still packed in the van. I took some ibuprofen. I can go to work," Rachel said.

"Can you dial Flick and put it on speaker?" Gunner asked.

Rachel wasn't sure why he needed Flick, but she did what he asked.

"Hello," Flick said.

"Hey, Rachel's got cramps. What were those warming things you had me buy for Beth that one time?" Gunner asked.

"They're thermal patches that keep the muscles warm. After we ran out a couple months ago, I ordered enough for the next two years for any woman on the compound. They're in the hall closet of our house. I'm on shift but feel free to get as many as you want. Sorry she's not feeling well. The stash of period chocolate is in the locked tote on the floor because otherwise, those sneaky dogs would get it open. Key is hanging on the wall of the same closet. Gotta go, we're getting called out," Flick said, hanging up.

Rachel stared at Gunner long enough and he finally sighed loudly.

"What?" he asked.

"You told Flick I had cramps," Rachel said.

"Well, yeah, he made me go buy Beth those thermal things when I lived with them. I knew he'd have what you needed," Gunner said.

Rachel tried to reconcile Gunner's blasé attitude about feminine issues with how her husband had acted. Her husband had been even more of an asshat than she knew.

"Thank you," Rachel said.

"No problem. I'm getting the thermal things for if you want them later today or tomorrow. After we get them and some of the chocolate, you're going home to relax on the couch with a heating pad, either to read or watch TV, got it?" Gunner asked.

"Yes, sir," Rachel smarted back.

"Hmmm, I like the sound of that, but let's table that discussion until you're feeling one hundred percent," Gunner quipped.

Oh my! She may feel like crap, but Gunner's words had her wondering if, just maybe, he was the perfect man for her.

CHAPTER ELEVEN

Gunner pulled the apple tarts out of the oven. He and Rachel had spent the last week working through how everything would be set up and how to situate the make-your-own bookmark station. Yesterday, they'd decided to ask for volunteers to run through some of the options before their opening next month.

Rachel had set up two craft stations. Some of the books she'd ordered were on the shelf but not all. A large delivery was coming next week, and there were at least ten boxes sitting in their office that needed to be added to inventory and put on the shelf.

He'd had to chuckle a little at the mulish face Rachel had given him after they'd picked up the thermal packs, and he'd taken her back home.

He'd gone into the house with her, then dug through the van until he found her heating pad.

He'd left her with the admonishment to rest and to text him what she'd like for lunch. Just to be a smart-ass, she'd texted pizza with mushrooms, beef and black olives. He'd gone to the clubhouse kitchen and whipped up a homemade pizza along with some garlic bread. The shock on her face when he brought her the homemade meal had him wondering if her husband had ever done any-thing nice.

Rachel had felt better by Tuesday, and they'd accomplished a lot this week, including him call-ing the Saint's Outlaws MC for help. He and Rachel had talked through what had happened with Justice's wife, Adley, who was a criminal lawyer but said she had some colleagues she would check with for availability. Gunner had also re-quested a *Get Well* delivery from Ruthy's Flower Shop if the Saint's Outlaws MC could find her husband. He might not have explained to Rachel that a *Get Well* delivery wasn't actually flowers, but a beatdown delivered by one of the Saint's

Outlaws MC members. He didn't lie because she didn't ask any questions about it.

He plated the tarts and brought them out to the counter. Instead of checking people out, all the food was laid on top of the cases for them to help themselves.

Two little people who'd burrowed into his heart more with each interaction ran over.

"Those smell good," Marcus said. Chelle nodded beside him.

"You can have some as soon as the filling cools a little. It would burn your mouth if you bit into them right now," Gunner cautioned.

"Okay, I'm going to…"

"It is I, Prospect Finn, tasked with fighting for the rights of majestic unicorns. How may I be of service to the realm?" Finn asked.

Gunner laughed along with everyone else. Finn had his pink unicorn and rainbow backpack slung over his shoulder and was waiting for his instructions.

Phoebe walked over to Finn and whispered something. He knelt down on the floor by her, putting his hand over his heart and whispering something back. What Gunner wouldn't give to know what Phoebe had said.

Gunner tested the heat of the tarts.

"Okay, they're good if you want to take them to share with everyone," Gunner said. Marcus grinned and picked up the tray.

Finn walked over, laying his backpack down. "I'm at your disposal for whatever you need done."

"First, I'm going to need to know what Phoebe said and who added the penalty of having to announce yourself like that," Gunner asked, motioning Finn to follow him into the kitchen.

"Phoebe said that I should learn from my mistakes and never disrespect one of her friends," Finn said, walking over and washing his hands.

"You mean, Phoebe came up with that for you to say and convinced someone to add it to the penalty?" Gunner asked, handing Finn a bowl of chocolate cookies to roll in powdered sugar.

"Yep. I guess she gave her idea to Bear and he called War. Since it came from the kids, War tacked it on to the penalty. You can guarantee I'm going to watch my words from now on," Finn muttered.

Gunner chuckled. "Good idea. Finish those, bake them for 12 minutes, then remove. After that, you can be in charge of drinks tonight."

Gunner headed out to the front and found Phoebe. "High-five, Pheebs. I'm proud of you for standing up for your friends."

Phoebe grinned that mischievous smile that he rarely saw her without. Man, with Chelle having friends like Phoebe, maybe he needed to propose a bigger fence at the compound. Who knows who Phoebe might irritate by the time she was in high school?

Rachel waved goodbye to Roam, Sprite, and her children. It was late. Sprite said she would take

Marcus and Chelle to Rachel's house to get them started on baths.

Rachel and Gunner had a few things to pick up before they closed for the night. The kids had adored their craft area. The build-your-own bookshelf area and decorate-your-own bookmark were a success.

Sprite had suggested having the kids' supplies in some divided containers that she used at the shop. She'd had Roam go grab an extra from Bluff Creek Ink. Sprite had shown Rachel how she would use it to set up the supplies. Rachel had loved it and ordered some right away.

Everyone had also voted on their favorite names for the cats. Now she could get tags made and have them ready to go.

As she put the supplies away, she thought about how close she'd grown to the women in the week since she'd arrived. Regina had helped her find a therapist for the kids to talk to about their bad daddy. He'd gotten them in for a first appointment. Chelle and Marcus had come to her separately and said they liked talking with him because he made them feel better.

Beth, Emerson, and the group, as Rachel had taken to calling them, couldn't quit talking about Rachel's overalls. She'd taken the Broken Hearts Brewing logo and made patches and iron-on transfers with it. She'd applied a large one to the front of her overalls and then had smaller ones all over the legs. She'd been pretty proud of herself that everyone loved them so much.

"Are you about finished?" Gunner asked as he locked the front door.

"Yes, give me five more minutes," she said.

"All right. I'll check the bathrooms, then meet you in the kitchen," Gunner said.

Rachel straightened the bookmark and book-shelf area. She stared at the bookcase and couldn't wait until they unloaded all the books onto the shelves. She and Gunner had set the book organi-zation get-together for February seventh because they were still waiting on some cartons of books. She didn't want to put the books they had up and then completely have to rearrange when the last ones came in.

She slid a chair under the table and deemed the room good enough for them to go home. She walked into the kitchen. Gunner was standing by the door, a smile on his face and wearing those thigh-hugging jeans he seemed to prefer. A tight black T-shirt was tucked into his jeans. The fabric outlined the muscles under it.

She swallowed, then realized she'd been staring at him longer than was appropriate.

"You ready?" she asked, walking up to him. His height and the way he treated her made her feel feminine and wondering what his lips would feel like.

"I've been ready for this for a week," Gunner growled, grasping her strap and tugging her closer. His breath, smelling of the bowl of candy mints he kept in the kitchen, wafted closer before warm lips claimed hers.

For a second, she was stunned but this was Gunner. His lips coaxed a response—not tentative but tempting her to let go. He wanted her full participation, and he was willing to wait.

She slid her hand up until her palm could cup his cheek. He was everything she imagined and more. Instead of being the bystander like she'd been her whole life, she dove into showing him she wanted whatever he was willing to give.

A low groan came from him. His hand slid down, grasping her bottom, tugging her tighter until she could feel every inch of his hardness against her. He made love to her mouth as if he couldn't get enough. There was no other word for how he was making her feel besides craved.

His lips coasted toward her neck, sending shivers down her spine. Her breasts felt heavy. She wanted to rub them against Gunner, but they had layers between them.

"More," she whispered. She wasn't sure what more she wanted or how far she wanted to go but she ached.

Gunner unhooked one of her straps, then lifted her onto the prep table. He stared into her eyes as his fingers unbuttoned the buttons at her hip.

His fingers slipped under her T-shirt, dragging it above her breasts.

"Yes?" he asked.

She nodded because she needed more. His finger traced her breast. Gunner dragged her bra cup down, revealing her hardened nipple. As tiny and slender as she was, she'd always wanted bigger breasts, but the grin on Gunner's face before he licked his tongue across the tip told her he was plenty happy with them.

The first touch had her arching. When he sucked hard, the pleasure shot straight between her legs. She widened her legs, wiggling, trying to get closer. He held her up while he ravished her breasts, slipping back and forth between them until she wanted to scream at him to take her.

His free hand slipped through the opening of her overalls, trailing across her stomach, sending more heat to her core.

She couldn't think as he found her center, rubbing and touching until everything inside her tightened. Her orgasm ripped through her.

She breathed deeply, trying to catch her breath. She opened her eyes to a smirk on Gunner's face. He brought the fingers he'd had inside her to his mouth, tasting her. *What exactly does one say? Thanks for the orgasm? Thanks for making me feel loved and worshipped?*

"Thank you," Gunner said, fixing her clothes.

"For?" she asked.

"Trusting me enough to let me bring you pleasure. It will hold me over until the day you're ready for me to remove every stitch of your clothes and sink inside you," he said, helping her off the table.

"Umm, when will I be ready?" Rachel asked. She'd felt his hardness. He wasn't pushing to have her right now. Gunner adjusted himself before flicking the lights off. She'd never met a man who was willing to wait.

"When you're ready to be mine and only mine forever," Gunner replied, leading her out to his bike.

CHAPTER TWELVE

Gunner was having the hardest time not laughing. He'd invited Rachel, Marcus, and Chelle to visit the farm area of the compound and to have lunch at the diner. In the last week, they'd made major headway on the shop. He, Rachel and the kids had spent most of the evenings together eating supper and playing games. Then, at bedtime, he helped put the kids to bed and kissed Rachel goodnight before heading back to the clubhouse.

He and Rachel were going to work later in the day, but this morning was about spending time with Rachel and the kids. He didn't have just Rachel to convince but also Marcus and Chelle.

Since they'd all left the house walking toward the farm area, Marcus and Chelle had been discussing all the animals Phoebe and Blake had at their houses. For the last five minutes, Marcus had been reciting facts about how much having an animal helped with overall health.

"And did you know that pets are a natural antidepressant? Seventy percent of pet owners report less loneliness, which would be good for you, Mom. Chelle and I are at school all day. It must be lonely for you," Marcus said.

Gunner fought the laughter. Rachel was working hard to keep her face calm but after being around the kids, Gunner didn't believe Rachel was lonely while they were at school. It was a break from the noise and chaos.

"It is different when you're at school, but I run our craft business. And now, I'll be working full-time at the coffee shop. I would think that it might not be fair to an animal to leave them alone all day," Rachel said.

"Mom, that's why Phoebe, Blake, and Benji suggested we ask for two. Then they can keep each other company when we're all gone," Chelle cajoled with a smile on her face.

"Oh, they did, did they? Any thoughts, Gunner?" Rachel asked.

"I did have pets growing up, and I agree with them being a great support. I also remember when my mom let us boys get puppies. They weren't trained to go outside to the bathroom yet. Brody, Flick, and I had to play rock, paper, scissors on who had to clean the poop off the floor," Gunner said, shuddering.

"Ewww," Chelle said.

"I know. Animals are a huge investment of time, but the plus is that because you live at Bluff Creek now, you have all these animals to visit," Gunner said, opening the barn door. The kids ran in while Rachel paused.

"Thank you. I'm not quite ready to add another thing that needs to be taken care of yet," she whispered.

He slid his arm around her shoulder. "I've got your back," he whispered close to her ear. And yep, seeing her little shiver had him running multiplication tables in his head. Nope, he was not getting hard for her in the barn. Marcus and

Chelle were way too inquisitive. Gunner was not ready for why his dick was hard in his jeans, nor the sex talk with the kids.

"Mama, Gunner, hurry up. There's a cat with kittens in here," Chelle yelled.

He followed behind Rachel, trying not to stare at her butt cupped in her overalls. He needed to get his dick to go down, not get harder. He'd never been around any woman who wore overalls, but he was a huge fan of them now.

"Why are they in with the donkey?" Chelle asked, trying to climb on the gate to Sourdough's stall.

"I don't know. Maybe the cat is friends with the donkey," Gunner said.

"Someone dropped them off at the front gate in a box. I brought them into the barn and put them in the empty stall on the end last night. Now they're in Sourdough's stall. Maybe they feel safe?" Baron said, walking over by the kids.

"Wait, someone just put them in a box and got rid of them?" Marcus asked.

Baron shrugged his shoulders, "Yes, sometimes people don't understand how much work animals are. We have to feed them, keep their stalls clean, and make sure they have fresh water. This time of year, we also have to check the outdoor water and break the ice off the top if it freezes."

Marcus scowled. "That's a lot of work."

"It is but they are worth it. And they really appreciate when you kids come visit them. Sourdough, here," Baron said, clicking his tongue.

Gunner adored the awe on Marcus and Chelle's faces as Sourdough came closer. Baron showed them her favorite spot to be rubbed. The kids deserved to experience every special moment in their lives, and if he had his way, he'd be the one to help make it happen.

"Do you want to play with the pigs?" Baron asked.

"Pigs?" Chelle squealed. He loved her dearly, but he had no idea young voices could hit that note.

"Yep," Baron said, leading them to another stall.

"The one that is a darker pink color is Baby Back Ribs, and the other is Pork Chop," Baron said.

"We're not going to eat them, are we?" Marcus asked. The green tinge to his cheeks had Gunner hoping Marcus wasn't going to throw up.

"Oh no. These are pets. They were sent to the rescue because someone thought they were getting mini pigs and they grew bigger than the person wanted. I got them for Regina," Baron said.

Gunner stood beside Rachel, his arm almost itching to slide around her shoulders. He gave in to the temptation and slid it around her. She turned toward him, smiled, and leaned against him.

If Flick would have described the warm feeling washing over him from holding his woman, Gunner would have not believed him. But today with Rachel, he was experiencing it for himself.

Why did having her by his side make him feel he could accomplish anything?

Rachel listened to the kids pepper Gunner with so many questions. After finishing at the farm, they'd headed to the diner. Since they'd sat down, her kids hadn't given him a break.

He didn't get irritated or shush them, which they'd experienced before. He took them one by one and answered them. A couple times when he hadn't known the answer, he'd admitted he hadn't been here long enough. Instead of ignoring what he didn't know, he'd called Flick, which had Flick and Beth joining them. He'd also asked Slice a question. Ten minutes later, Slice's wife, Faith, with their kids had shown up.

The look on her kids' faces when Isaiah, Micah, and Deborah had sat down was priceless. Of course, Faith had asked Rachel if she wanted to hold their one-year-old, and Rachel had jumped at the chance. He was sitting on her lap, picking up the little pieces of food Faith had cut up for him.

She was in a diner with her kids and people she'd met a couple weeks ago. She was closer to them than she'd ever been with her family. This feeling for the family she'd found was something she'd always dreamed of.

There was that one niggling issue that was keeping her from giving Gunner the green light and opening up her heart fully.

"Having deep thoughts?" Beth asked.

Rachel nodded. She didn't want to share in front of everyone, especially the kids, but she did need some advice.

"How about after we all finish lunch, you, Faith, and I can go chat? Flick, Slice, and Gunner could take the kids to the park while we talk," Beth offered.

"I think that would be a good idea," Rachel said. She had an idea, but it would help if she had some other opinions. Sometimes when she was in a situation, she couldn't see all the moving pieces.

"Trust me. Whatever your issue, we can figure it out. If I think it's more involved, we'll enlist some of the others. I consider you a friend, Rachel. You,

Gunner, and the kids look happy together. I'll do anything that's needed to make that be permanent for you. If that's what you want," Beth said.

Rachel nodded because her throat was too full to speak. Meeting Clara online must have been fate because since coming to Bluff Creek, Rachel had been welcomed, accepted, and given the chance to think of what she truly wanted.

She glanced over at Gunner. He must have felt her eyes on him because he turned toward her and winked. How the heck could his wink convey so much to her?

She was going to meet with Beth, and they were going to get her situation figured out. She had a beautiful life that she deserved to experience with Gunner.

CHAPTER THIRTEEN

Gunner had fun hanging with the kids and then working with Rachel. He'd discussed his idea with Rachel, and she'd adored it.

Now he was waiting for his victims—well brothers in the brotherhood—to show up and help him out.

"Okay, I'm here. The party can start," Dex called as he and Halligan walked in.

"You didn't say it was a council meeting, so Dex said I could tag along," Halligan said.

"Hey, the more the merrier," Gunner said. He wondered if they'd all be so excited when they heard what he had planned. He had gotten his President on board because it never hurt to have an ace in the hole.

War, Roam, Flick, Brody, Scoop, and Stone walked in together. The line of bikes parked out front was growing.

"Cannon said he'd be here but had to fish something out of the toilet that Hank had dropped," War said.

"While we're waiting, I've got ice-cold beers here and snacks if you want to eat," Gunner said.

Roam walked over and snagged a beer. "I feel like you're trying to bribe us," he said.

War chuckled, grabbing a couple and passing them out.

Baron, Rascal, and Locks walked in together.

"Did we miss it?" Locks asked.

"Miss what?" Stone asked.

"I haven't got to see Finn riding the motorbike or announcing himself when he comes in. I didn't want to miss it," Locks said.

Stone snickered, taking a sip of his beer.

"You never laugh like that. What did you do?" Rascal asked, sitting down.

"I drained the gas from it to make sure everyone had time to get here," Stone said.

"Nice job," Scoop said.

"I might have also added some modifications to his helmet. I thought the penalty wasn't quite enough," Stone said.

Gunner handed out plates and napkins, then passed around the trays of snacks.

"I have dessert after we finish our activity tonight," Gunner said.

"Activity sounds ominous when you don't explain anything," Baron said.

Gunner shrugged. Nope, he wasn't sharing yet.

Slice, Bear, Cannon, and Ben walked in.

"Dumbass is about two blocks behind us," Ben said.

Gunner directed them to the beers. This was going to be a long three months for Finn, but maybe he'd think twice before he ran his mouth off.

Instead of the throaty growl of a Harley, the buzzing sound of a motorbike came closer and Finn pulled up. Gunner shook his head at all of the men pulling out their phones to video. When he saw the modifications Stone had made, he chuckled along with everyone else. Finn's helmet now sported a unicorn horn, and the back fender of the bike had what Gunner thought looked like a unicorn tail made from plastic.

Finn walked in and paused at everyone waiting on him.

"Fuck…" he groaned. "It is I, Prospect Finn, tasked with fighting for the rights of majestic unicorns. How may I be of service to the realm?" Finn asked.

"You can take off your hat so we can properly see you," Ben said, laughing between the words.

"I knew it had to be you," Finn yelled, running toward Ben.

Chairs scraped as everyone got up to keep the brothers from brawling.

"Stop! If you two want to fight, we can make a time, but you're not going to damage anything in the business. We're here to complete a project for Gunner. Suck it up and quit acting like children," War said.

When both men nodded, everyone calmed down and sat down. War grabbed the hat off of

Finn before he sat down, which had everyone laughing again. Finn's short blonde hair was now a pink color.

"Gunner, let's get started," War said.

"Okay, I'd like your help with Valentine's cards. Since we're opening right before Valentine's and the shop is Broken Hearts Brewing, I want to have Valentine's cards available for everyone who comes in the first week. I also asked Regina for a list of widows or widowers who lost their person in the last year. I'll be sending them a note with an invitation to come to our opening. I also want the cards available for anyone who has had a breakup to pick up," Gunner said.

He looked around the room. He didn't pick up any negativity about doing the activity.

"Sounds good. Any specifications for what we write?" Stone asked.

Gunner grinned as everyone started discussing what would be best and taking the supplies Gunner had laid out. He should have known he didn't have anything to worry about since the activity was for others.

He stared at Finn with the pink hair. He wondered if they should have someone dressed up for the holiday—not necessarily Cupid, but maybe something unique to Broken Hearts. He texted what he was pondering to Rachel. She could start thinking about it and they could brainstorm together.

Gunner refilled the food trays and then sat down to write a couple cards. This chapter of his life was coming together, but he was itching to move to the next. He would have never believed he could be all in so quickly.

"Hey, Gunner, do you have any more trash cans or buckets for the paper scraps? I hate to make more work for you because we're all messy," Brody said.

"Yeah, let me go grab some. I have some in the smash room," Gunner said. He appreciated Brody thinking of his time and wanting to help. Honestly, he'd been worried that Brody would do something to the store, but then he realized Brody wasn't that juvenile.

He pushed the door open and was immediately covered in something wet and cold. He looked at the gelatinous chunks on his arms and his shirt. He knew immediately what had happened.

"Brody," Gunner bellowed.

"Payback is hell. Now we're even. You leave me alone and I'll leave you alone," Brody said.

Gunner turned—all the guys were in the hallway. Half of them were videoing him. Gunner nodded. He'd call a truce for now. But once the store was open, it would be open season again.

Tonight, Marcus and Chelle both had friends staying over with them. The kids had beamed when she'd told them the plans.

Rachel got to have a fun evening while the kids had friends over too. Clara, Regina, Meg, Beth, and Jesse had come over to hang out and crochet. Clara and Meg were helping Rachel make some more of the cats. Beth was making hand-crocheted blankets, and Jesse was learning from her.

She'd giggled, laughed, and talked while they worked on crafts together. When Meg had mentioned Bluff Creek Crafts & Things had times people could meet to craft, Rachel added to her list of things she wanted to do in Bluff Creek.

"So I heard the kids were trying to convince you to get an animal," Regina said softly.

Rachel appreciated her keeping it quiet.

"Oh my gosh, do you know how many times I've heard the same facts about loneliness and how pets help alleviate it?" Rachel whispered back.

"It's still too chilly right now to get a new animal that you'd have to take outside to pee," Beth replied.

"I have to admit that this morning wasn't my proudest mom moment when Marcus would not shut up about getting two so they could be friends. I basically said that until we'd been here at least two months, we would not even discuss it. Of course, it could have been because I was in the shower with the music on and thought I might get maybe five minutes to myself," Rachel said.

"I think that's a good way to do it. You didn't say no but gave them a timeline for when you will be willing to discuss. If I wouldn't have been so overwhelmed with all the love the guys and Baron were showing my boys, I would have screamed when Baron bought them German Shepherd puppies that first Christmas. But everyone helped with them, and my boys had done without for so long that I was ecstatic the way the men in the MC embraced all of us. You can always take one of the farm animals for an overnight. The bunnies are good for something like that," Regina said.

Rachel finished her cat, adding the nose and eyes. She put it in the pile and picked out some different color yarn.

"I love your idea for the cats and everything else. Do you and Gunner need help getting all the books on the shelves? I'd love to help," Jesse said.

Beth snickered, "Oh, but don't expect her to work too fast. If her kids are all at home, she'll probably read the back of each book before putting it on the shelf."

"Well, of course. I adore the twins and Hank. Finding time to read a book, let alone peruse the synopsis, doesn't happen very often. The girls just started walking and they are so fast. Now, not that they need to reach for anything because if they make a sound, Hank is there trying to get them whatever they need," Jesse said.

"Aww, he's such a sweet older brother," Clara said.

Jesse giggled. "Can you imagine how he's going to act when they start dating? He and Cannon will probably run off every boy who comes over."

"Oh yes, they will. Think about my Ariel. War and Baron were even keeping tabs on her as an adult," Regina said.

"How'd that turn out?" Rachel asked.

"Oh, she's married to Pit, the Saint's Outlaw MC President, but War didn't make it easy," Regina said.

Rachel enjoyed the conversations and crafting with the women. Gunner's text about Finn's pink hair making him think about the pink cats she was making had her smiling.

"Oh, that smile has to be about a man," Meg said.

"Gunner sent me something to think about for the shop," Rachel replied. She liked these women but what she and Gunner had was new. She still had the issue to deal with. Beth had updated her that the plan was in motion, but no updates were available yet. She only hoped it worked out the way she wanted.

She wasn't sure what she'd do if it failed. For once in her life, she was going to hope for exactly what she wanted—not just take whatever life handed her and live with it, keeping a smile on her face. Beth had told Rachel that she needed to dream. Rachel decided that was what she was going to do—dream of a life here at Bluff Creek with a certain chef. A chef who she wouldn't mind licking more than the beaters from his creation he let her lick a couple of days ago.

CHAPTER FOURTEEN

Gunner held Rachel's hand as they walked into Nelson's Honkytonk Saloon & Bar for the party. Since Broken Hearts Brewing had a huge Valentine's event planned, Bluff Creek had decided to have a night out in Dodge City two weeks before their grand opening.

The kids were having a huge sleepover at the gym with Baron, Regina, Hope, Locks, Meg, Rascal, and Clara overseeing the party. Since the kids from Nelson's were attending too, Hennessy and Ellie's older kids were helping babysit along with Deborah. They had a bounce house, movie marathon, and crafts planned.

Gunner planned on using this time to dance with Rachel and see if she was ready for more.

They'd spent this week much like last week—working together and spending evenings as a family.

The only dark spot on the horizon was that none of the Saint's Outlaws had been able to find Maynard to deliver Gunner's *Get Well* delivery. Scoop said he wasn't using credit cards.

"Over here," Jesse yelled from a group of tables pushed together.

Gunner was ready to sit back and enjoy time with his woman. Good food and drink plus some up close and personal time on the dance floor.

Although he adored Rachel's overalls, tonight she'd dressed in tight jeans, boots, and a leather jacket for the ride. Standing by the table, he waited for Rachel to take off the jacket.

Oh Friggin' fudgesicles. The front of her shirt was silky with a high neck, but it was the back that was going to kill him. The silky fabric trailed down to the top of her butt, which would be fine if there wasn't a huge diamond opening in the back with no hint of a bra strap. Was his woman bare beneath her shirt?

How was he supposed to concentrate tonight wondering if anything was underneath her top?

"Oh, the top looks perfect on you," Beth said as they settled in their seats.

"Thank you. I appreciate you loaning it to me," Rachel said.

"Anytime you want to try something different, let me know. I have a whole room full of clothes for surveillance," Beth said, passing plates, forks, and a tray of appetizers their way.

Gunner listened to the conversation, enjoying being here with Rachel. He couldn't wait to open Broken Hearts Brewing, but tonight, where he and Rachel weren't in charge of providing the food and service, was just what they both needed to recharge.

"Hey, Gunner, you guys have all your positions filled at the coffee shop?" Hennessy asked.

"We have a start but we're waiting to see how many we'll need on some of the shifts. For now, some of the workers from the diner are going to help out during heavy times. Why?" Gunner asked.

"Elijah and Morgan are interested in part-time jobs. We're letting them learn at the oil office but both of them wanted some experience in the food industry. We can't have them working here since we serve liquor. I didn't know if you might need extra help on the weekends," Hennessy said.

"Let Rachel and I check the schedule but as long as it hasn't been promised to someone already, I'd love to have them working on the weekends. I have a feeling the smash room will be busy," Gunner replied.

"Thanks, man," Hennessy said.

Gunner ate some of the appetizers and refilled Rachel's plate when it was empty. Seeing her eyes light up and her grin gave him such a sense of satisfaction.

A slow song came on the jukebox. Gunner leaned close to Rachel. "Would you like to dance?" he asked.

"Yes," she said, grasping his hand.

Leading her onto the dance floor was a good thing because he couldn't see the deep V of bare flesh but when she turned toward him to dance, he realized the error in his thinking.

He pulled her close to dance. His hand was on bare skin. He swallowed, reminding himself he had all night.

"Just in case you're wondering, the top has a built-in bra," Rachel said, smirking up at him. He wanted to pick her up, let her wrap her legs around him, and kiss her until they forgot their names.

"Seems like you're feeling a little sassy. I like seeing this side of you," Gunner said.

Rachel followed his lead. He hadn't realized how much he needed to hold her and be in the moment.

"Since this is your first time at Nelson's, I should probably warn you. The Nelson cousins are a tad wild. I've yet to be here that some type of excitement hasn't happened," Gunner said, breathing in the light, fresh fragrance Rachel wore.

"Umm, what type of excitement?" she asked.

"Usually someone doesn't treat an employee or customer nicely and they boot them from the bar.

It's always interesting to see which brother wins on doing the honors," Gunner said.

"I think I'm going to like this place," Rachel said, leaning her head against his chest as the song segued into a slow song.

Feeling Rachel against him had him fighting his body's response. Every time he placed a little space between them to try to regain control of his pulse-pounding dick, she shifted closer.

He glanced down at her face. Her lips were tilted up in a smirk.

"Are you teasing me on purpose? I'm trying to be a gentleman on the dance floor when every move you make is making me harder than steel," Gunner whispered in her ear, enjoying her tremble at his words.

"Of course," she said.

Gunner paused on the dance floor. She nudged him.

"Keep dancing," she whispered. He danced with her, thinking about how far she'd come and how comfortable she'd sounded saying she was teasing him.

"Yo, keep moving. No sex on the dance floor," Halligan said as he danced by with a woman Gunner didn't recognize.

"If you think that's what sex is, I feel really sorry for your dates, Halligan," Rachel replied.

Yep, she was feeling sassy tonight, and he adored this side of her. She always had a smile on her face, but she wasn't putting on a brave face. She truly was happy.

Rachel walked into her house with Gunner. His touches on the dance floor, then being on the bike with him, had every part of Rachel hungering for Gunner.

She paused by the closet, taking off her jacket and hanging it up. She'd only been with Maynard. She wasn't sure how to move them from here to being closer.

Gunner's finger traced along her spine, sliding down her back. He moved her hair away from her neck. His warm breath on the side of her neck had her leaning back against him. His arms wrapped around her. His hand slid under her shirt, resting above her waistband.

"We can just sit and watch a movie or do some heavy petting on the couch. I don't want to rush you," Gunner said softly.

She thought about since she'd come to Bluff Creek a little over three weeks ago. Each day, Gunner had shared a little more of himself until she couldn't deny how she felt for him.

It was more than like and so much more than just an infatuation. Her situation wasn't resolved, but as far as she was concerned, the papers granting her a divorce were a formality. She and Maynard had ceased to be a couple when he left her and the kids the first time.

Gunner needed the words because she didn't want any miscommunication between them.

"You aren't rushing me," she said, turning toward him and looking into his eyes. "You are who

I want. Will you take me to bed and make me yours?" she whispered.

She barely had time to see the smile spreading across Gunner's face before he picked her up and carried her toward the bedroom.

"I will because I can't get you off my mind," Gunner said, pausing at the foot of the bed. He claimed her lips, the warm, familiar touch and taste of Gunner giving her the feeling of home she'd been looking for her whole life.

Gunner divested them of their clothes while kissing each part of her he uncovered. Somewhere during that, he took his clothes off until she could feel the roughness of his leg hair rasping against her thighs.

He paused, notched at her entrance. "I have to say this because I don't want you to think it's part of that after-sex glow. I love you. I've loved you since you smiled and introduced your kids. I know people say it can't happen that fast, but it did. I fell for you, and it's only deepened over the time we're together. I love you and I'm making you mine," Gunner said.

Rachel was trying to formulate a reply when Gunner breached her opening. His eyes screamed everything he felt for her as he made her his. She so wanted to tell him she loved him too, but with every touch and thrust he was making her forget her own name.

All she could think of was touching him as she let him drive her higher until her legs were wrapped around his waist and she was screaming his name. His lips claimed hers as he followed her over.

She basked in the moment of being one with the man she'd fallen for before she gave him the words.

"The first time I started opening my heart to you was when you took us to the diner for breakfast and made sure the kids had fun. Then you put your own wants aside to make sure Marcus could get the help he needed by telling me what Maynard had said. Holding me as I broke down and had snot all over my face, I knew that you were someone I could trust. Each time we talked or spent time with the kids, you showed me the man you are. I love you. It wasn't a flash bang, but it was a slow build until every part of my life is filled with the love you give me. This isn't a sex afterglow. This is me telling the man who just made love to me that I love you too," Rachel said, her voice quivering.

Gunner cupped her face. "I love you so much. I'm so thankful you came to Bluff Creek. Let me take care of this condom then I want to fix you a dessert. We'll need fuel for the next round," he said.

So he not only worshipped her in bed, but he also wanted to cook for her to refuel. Yes, she'd found a keeper.

CHAPTER FIFTEEN

Rachel lay looking at Gunner beside her in bed. He was on his back with the sheet around his waist. The tattoos on his arm and chest were tempting her to trace them with her tongue. But the rise of his cock underneath the sheet had her wanting her mouth on something else.

They'd gone to the kitchen last night for Gunner to cook. They'd only made it as far as him mixing up the fudge cake before her hands touching him had him saying, "Fuck it," grabbing a couple granola bars and some bottles of water.

For a woman who'd only known missionary, Gunner had opened up her world last night. After he wound her up by licking and worshipping every inch between her legs, he rolled over onto his back, slid a condom on, and told her to get on for a ride. She'd been so hesitant, but Gunner's hands on her hips, helping her get a rhythm, had given her confidence.

Gunner had made her feel sexy and had never made her feel inadequate because of her small breasts. The only thing she hadn't gotten to do that she wanted was suck on his cock. She moved down his body, slowly pulling the covers down past his cock. She leaned close, breathing in his musky scent. She tentatively licked the head, then down his shaft.

Gunner's groan had her smiling. His hand grasping her hair made her look up at him. His heavy-lidded gaze heated up every part of her.

"That's a really fantastic way to wake up," he said, his voice husky.

"How about this?" she said, getting up on her knees to get a better angle before she engulfed his cock.

"Oh, Rachel, honey," Gunner groaned.

Banging on the storm door had Rachel pulling off his cock.

"Did we lock the front door last night," Rachel whispered.

Gunner extricated them from the covers, jumping up. "Nope," he said, dragging on his jeans.

"How are we playing this?" Gunner asked.

Rachel just stared at him, not knowing what to say. She hadn't considered this.

"Mama, we're hiding from the boys," Chelle yelled.

Rachel ran to the door, closing and locking it. "Okay, Chelle, I need to get dressed. Who's with you?" she asked, staring at Gunner, trying to figure out how to handle this.

"Just Blake and Phoebe. We're hiding from Benji and Marcus. We're going to hide in the loft," Chelle yelled.

Rachel's shoulders relaxed. At least the kids hadn't seen bare flesh.

"They can't see your door from the loft. Do you want me to leave out the door to the garage or your back door? If you're not ready for them to know I spent the night, I'm fine with that. They need stability, and I'll do whatever you think is best," Gunner said softly.

Could this man be any more perfect?

Rachel slid her arms around him. "I think we need to prepare them and have an answer about Maynard because I don't want them to ever think I cheated on him."

"I agree. Let's get dressed. You can check for anyone else coming in. I'll go through the garage and out the side door. If anyone sees me, they'll think I was on a walk, especially since we left my bike at the clubhouse," he said, finishing dressing.

She slipped on clothes and didn't worry about brushing her hair or teeth yet. She slipped the door open and peeked out. The coast was clear.

"Thank you," she said, kissing his cheek.

"Thank you and to be continued," he said, grinning and slipping out the door to the garage.

The front door banged open as she turned around.

"Mama, have you seen Chelle?" Marcus asked.

"Why do you ask, and where are you supposed to be?" Rachel asked.

Her heart was calming down. She'd just have to give up on a leisurely morning in bed and then breakfast. She'd shower and then see if Regina or anyone needed help with Sunday lunch.

She wished she and Gunner would have had more time together. Besides wanting to finish what she started, she'd made the decision to share the plan she and Beth had put into motion. Maybe they could find time after lunch.

She couldn't wait for the day that Gunner would stay the night and there wouldn't be any hiding. She'd never had shower sex and was looking forward to experimenting with him. But on a deeper level, she missed him when he wasn't around. Each touch, each word he'd given her had shown her that she had nothing to fear and everything to gain.

CHAPTER SIXTEEN

Rachel paused unloading the books to sit down for a minute. Between the Franks sisters and the other women, she'd spent half the evening laughing. Gunner and some of the guys were playing with the kids at Beth and Flick's outdoor laser tag course. Marcus and Chelle had been so excited.

"So, you mean to tell me that you and War didn't like each other when he came back?" Frankie asked.

"Oh, he was a dick on an epic level. We had gotten crossways in high school, and he couldn't see the business owner I'd become, but sometimes the hardest roads bring the greatest adventures," Remi said.

"Blah, blah, blah, I don't want to hear how perfect your life is. Your child isn't walking yet and can't get into everything. We'll talk about the perfect road to love when you're pregnant and your children don't know the meaning of a closed door," Sprite whined.

"How about we have all the kids over so you and Roam can get ya some or bask in the lack of sounds in a kid-free house for a night?" Remi said.

"No takebacks," Sprite said, shelving some of the indie author books that Rachel had ordered in.

"I kind of did something that might blow up in all our faces," Jesse said, continuing to shelve books with her back to all of them.

"Blow up like let's get the guns out and start carrying with sentries outside of town or blow up because it might cause someone emotional trauma?" Regina asked.

"Umm, the latter like maybe a Code Rachel," Jesse said, turning to face the group.

"Come tell us about it," Meg said. Rachel marveled at how quickly everyone sat down around tables.

"Back in October, Cannon was having trouble sleeping. We talked about it. He'd been having dreams that he had other siblings out there who weren't in good situations. I bought us DNA tests to see if his dad had left any siblings somewhere. I didn't want Cannon to have to go through it alone, so I did one for myself too," Jesse said.

"Well, don't keep us in suspense. Does Cannon have more siblings out there?" Clara asked.

Rachel waited because she couldn't imagine where this was going.

"No. At least, not that we know of yet. But it came back that we have five possible cousins," Jesse said.

"But—" Winnie said, turning to Remi.

"Umm, I thought Mom and Dad were both only children. Neither of them ever brought up anything about siblings or parents. I assumed they were all gone," Remi said.

"Me too. So I guess we need to figure out if we want to contact them," Sarah said.

Beth shook her head. "Nope, Jesse wouldn't be worried if she hadn't already contacted them. What did you find out?"

"You did?" Sarah asked.

"I did. I saw the matches and contacted them each individually. The oldest replied," Jesse said.

"Well, what did she say?" Remi demanded.

"She's the oldest of five sisters. They're the daughters of Aaron Franks," Jesse said.

"And who is Aaron Franks?" Remi asked.

"I don't know. I was going to ask Dad, but I figured that I better ask soon because I invited them to visit Bluff Creek and Broken Hearts Brewing for our grand opening," Jesse said.

When the conversation turned into an argument, Regina suggested maybe the girls should all sleep on what they'd found out before they said something they'd regret to each other. The sisters were divided on what needed to happen and accepted Regina's suggestion.

Rachel was glad they were toward the end of unloading the boxes because the tension between the sisters was unnerving her.

"We have about forty-five minutes until my children will be returned. My primary goal would be getting the rest of the books unloaded. They've already been scanned into our system for inventory tracking. I really appreciate all the help you've given me," Rachel said.

Clara slid her arm around Rachel. "I'm glad you decided to come here."

"Me too," Rachel said, hugging Clara back.

The little disagreement between the sisters, though unnerving, had been a good thing. Getting to see family disagree but still get along was something new for Rachel. Her dad and mom hadn't allowed any disagreements. They hadn't allowed any deviation from what they considered appropriate. Over the years, Rachel had second-guessed her decision to keep the kids away from her parents and never trying to introduce them to their grandkids, but after seeing the way family worked at Bluff Creek, she'd come to the realization she'd made the right decision. This was the type of family she wanted her kids to experience.

Gunner had brought the kids to the store. He'd planned on the four of them spending a little bit of time together before heading home. But Roam had called that he needed help with something at Bluff Creek Ink. Gunner had run over to help out and was headed back.

He decided to take the back way and walk through the alley. He'd wanted to check the sensor on the outdoor motion lights and now was the perfect time. Although there was a large light in the lot, it didn't illuminate their back door or the area where their dumpster was located. He listened to the night sounds, thinking about how cute Marcus and Chelle had been coming back to the store. Marcus had been ecstatic that he and

Benji had finished first one of the rounds. Chelle had said she had fun playing with everyone.

Despite what they'd gone through, both kids had such sweet personalities. The parking lot was dark except for directly around the large light. He walked toward the back door. It only took a couple seconds to trigger the motion light. One less thing to worry about. He unlocked the back door and walked into the kitchen. It was quiet but then he heard talking.

It wasn't that he planned on eavesdropping, but the kids were asking questions that caught his attention.

"Mama, what is Gunner?" Chelle asked.

"I don't think I understand the question," Rachel replied.

"Well, Roam is Blake's dad but we gots bad daddy still. What is Gunner?" Chelle asked.

"I don't want to see bad daddy ever again," Marcus said.

Gunner's stomach clenched at the worry in Marcus' voice. Well, if he had anything to do with it, neither of the kids would ever be in bad daddy's presence again.

"Well, Gunner is someone special in our life right now. Later, he might be more but it's complicated," Rachel said.

Only because the kids' bad daddy was still hiding somewhere. If Gunner could get it resolved, things would become uncomplicated quickly. Only one hand had to work to sign divorce documents and relinquish rights to the kids.

"Do you think Gunner could be our dad?" Marcus asked.

"I wants Gunner. He makes me feel safe," Chelle said.

"I think Gunner would make a great dad, but like I said, it's complicated, and we'd have to ask him. But let's wait, okay?" Rachel said.

Gunner could work with that. Although he'd love to walk in and answer the question, he wasn't taking Rachel's power away from her. She told the kids she wanted to wait.

Gunner walked back to the back door, opening and closing it loudly.

"I'm back. Who wants to get dessert before bed?" Gunner called, walking into the room.

"Me, please!" Chelle and Marcus yelled, running toward him and throwing their arms around him. He wrapped his arms around these little ones that he was going to protect with his life if needed.

"Well, let's go. We don't want Slice to eat it all. I heard he made some apple cobbler and was thinking about not sharing," Gunner said.

"Mama, let's hurry," Marcus said, running to grab her hand.

"Okay, let's go eat," Rachel said, with that gorgeous smile on her face that Gunner adored.

He had a little time, but he wasn't waiting forever. Valentine's seemed the perfect time for something special.

CHAPTER SEVENTEEN

Rachel had a hard time not skipping through the store. Everything was coming together, and their soft opening was tonight. Despite all the things they'd been checking off their lists for the store, Gunner had made them dinner every night.

Monday night, he'd shown the kids how to make pizza crust, and they'd made pizza pockets, which both kids had loved. Marcus had asked if it was something he could make to take in his lunch to school. Gunner hadn't hesitated but immediately said yes.

Tuesday and Wednesday, he'd let the kids pick what he made. Tuesday had been hot dogs and French fries for Marcus, and Chelle had wanted macaroni and cheese with fresh bread.

With the soft opening tonight, Bear and Winnie had taken the girls, and Roam and Sprite had taken the boys. Rachel moved the cards Blake and Phoebe had made to make room to add the ones Benji had made. When Benji had brought his items in, it was all she and Gunner could do to keep a straight face.

Benji had decided to take some of the members of Bluff Creek's favorite sayings and make cards. She hadn't met Bootstrap yet, but when Regina had seen the Babygirl cards, she'd said they'd be flying off the shelves.

Although consignment or a sixty/forty split might be better for Broken Hearts Brewing, Rachel and Gunner thought fostering the kids' entrepreneurial spirit would be the best path to take. The kids were now part of Broken Hearts Brewing's entrepreneurship program. The kids received an immediate twenty-five percent of whatever they made to be sold upon delivering the product. Fifty percent would be put into an account and divided equally among all the kids who had items for sale in the business that month. The remaining twenty-five percent went to Broken Hearts Brewing's bottom line. If the store took off like she and Gunner anticipated, the remaining twenty-five percent would move into an account for bonuses for the kids and quarterly parties celebrating the wins while discussing what they could do to increase sales. It was just one more aspect of Bluff Creek that Rachel loved—their unwavering support of children.

"How's my gorgeous woman today? Are you ready for the horde of partiers?" Gunner asked, his hand sliding around her. She shivered at the touch of his lips on her neck. His hand turned her face up to taste her lips.

She turned around, sliding her hands behind his neck. They'd been so busy. Sure, he could have stayed over but she wanted to have that talk with the kids first. Between his touches in the kitchen while he fixed supper or here at the shop, he kept her need for him on a slow simmer.

"Did I tell you how much I adore your overalls?" Gunner asked.

"I don't think so. Why?" she asked.

"Because they're so cute and make getting access to you very easy," Gunner said, his panty-melting grin putting all sorts of dirty thoughts in her head.

"And when are you going to take advantage of their easy access?" she asked, tilting her head toward the bank of windows at the front of the store.

"You know, we have an office with very few windows," Gunner replied.

"Yes, we do," she murmured, tugging his head down for a kiss.

The slam of the door barely registered. Maybe whoever it was would come back.

"It is I, Prospect Finn, tasked with fighting for the rights of majestic unicorns. How may I be of service to the realm?" Finn asked.

Gunner pulled back just enough to growl, "Leave."

"Does that mean you don't want help from any of us?" Stone asked.

Gunner sighed against her, rolling his eyes. "To be continued," he said.

And wasn't that the mantra of every parent?

Rachel motioned Finn over to help her. She needed a couple things added to the top shelf.

"So I guess maybe we should rename Broken Hearts Brewing to the Horny Hearts Brewing," Stone said.

Gunner stared at his friend, wondering if Rachel would be irritated if he hit Stone a few times to relieve some of the frustration.

"Sometimes, I think I liked you better when you never talked," Gunner muttered.

Brody, Flick, and some of the kids walked in. "Put us to work," Brody said.

Gunner showed Brody the list and let him be in charge of things for everyone to do. As the oldest, Brody would keep everyone moving. Gunner had some more prep work and items to cook.

Despite having spent hours planning and organizing with Rachel, Gunner was still a little nervous about the soft opening. All their ideas had been pulled together. Now they needed to see if it all worked. Elijah and Morgan had spent time learning the machine for the drinks, including all the coffee flavors they offered. Gunner hoped that at some point they'd be roasting their own coffee beans but right now, they were only grinding and brewing.

With all the help, Gunner had the food and drink items ready with fifteen minutes to spare before their soft opening time. He straightened a couple of trays in the case, checked that the cash register had been loaded with money, and that the tablet was ready to accept card payments.

"I double-checked all the payments were ready to go. I filled out the sheet with our starting cash too and it's in the bank bag," Morgan said.

"Good job. I appreciate you taking care of that already. Do you feel comfortable with the register?" Gunner asked.

"Yes. Elijah and I are good. We're going to take turns every thirty to forty minutes and switch jobs. Slice and one of the employees from the diner are helping out too" Morgan replied.

Gunner patted him on the shoulder, glancing around for Rachel.

"She's showing Dex and Rascal the procedures for the smash room. They have first shift," Morgan said, pointing to a schedule on the counter.

He'd completely missed having a specific schedule for areas besides the food and drink. It was a good thing his woman was highly organized. He wove his way through the MC family, who were already drifting in. He wanted to make sure Rachel was out here for the first part of the evening.

He rounded the corner of the hallway and bumped into Rachel.

"Exactly the woman I was looking for," Gunner said, tugging her close for a hug. Her arms slipping around his waist settled something in him and his nerves quieted. He and Rachel had planned along with the brotherhood. Tonight would be fine.

"I'm so excited. Are you going to give an opening speech?" she asked.

"No. We're giving an opening speech," he said, taking her hand and leading her out front. He led her toward the door that had a closed sign and turned them to the crowd of their MC family. He whistled loudly to get their attention.

"I have a couple things to say before we open. When Beth mentioned one of her ideas to Flick and I overheard, I couldn't resist saying I was interested. It was a way for me to be a part of the MC and give back to the club. These last six and a half months have been amazing, getting to know everyone and becoming a part of the Bluff Creek family. But a month ago, my life got even better. A pixie-sized ray of sunshine and her two amazing kids walked into my life.

"I can't believe not only how well we work together but also how much she's brought to my life personally. But tonight is about business, and she's more than an employee. I know you'll want to go over the new benefit package with Roam, our Treasurer, before accepting but I hope you'll agree to be the new co-manager for Broken Hearts Brewing," Gunner said.

"I accept. I'm sure the package will be fine because since we've come here, the MC has been so generous. How could I not work with the man who shows me every day that the kids and I matter? Now, let's get these doors open and take care of our customers. I know exactly how much we need to make each month for a profit. And we have some kids who are invested in seeing their items sell," Rachel said, smiling her sweet smile up at him.

He nodded, flipped the neon open sign on, and opened the door.

"Welcome to Broken Hearts Brewing," Rachel said, as the line of people made their way in.

The soft opening included friends and family of the club that had been invited. Hopefully, things would be calm, and they could work through any issues with service before they opened officially on Saturday.

CHAPTER EIGHTEEN

Rachel refilled the station with the items from the kids. The cards were selling faster than she could put them out. Two women were fighting over the last Babygirl card until she let them know she had more in the back.

Because Rachel didn't know everyone invited to the soft opening, she didn't know if they'd been invited or possibly walked in when they saw the open sign. She and Gunner had said that if it looked like more people were coming than they'd anticipated, he'd put a brother at the door to keep their numbers under capacity for fire code.

When Rachel walked into the office, the Franks sisters were in there discussing something.

"Everything okay?" Rachel asked.

"I hope so. I really, really hope I didn't mess up the soft opening," Jesse said.

"Well, it's too late now. We'll deal with any consequences," Remi said, shrugging her shoulders.

"I had no idea that Dad would refuse to talk with me about it. I didn't even get a chance to tell him what I'd done before he stormed out of the room," Jesse said.

"Can I butt in?" Rachel asked.

"Of course, and you don't need to ask. Not only are we using your office but trust me, everyone butts into everything in Bluff Creek," Beth said.

"Your dad is one of the nicest men I've ever met. He might have been mad when you asked because it brought up bad memories. I bet when they get here, he'll come around," Rachel said.

She hoped that was what happened. The Franks sisters had been so nice, and she wanted this to be a good experience for them. New cousins sounded exciting.

"Hey, sunshine, you ladies need to get out here. I believe the SUV with five women and three kids that just parked across the street are your special guests," Bear said, smirking at Winnie.

"Well, let's go face the music, ladies. If anything bad happens, we'll pay to fix everything," Sarah promised.

Rachel hurried out. She was not missing a minute of this. She caught Gunner's gaze and motioned toward the women walking toward the building. A tall brunette was in a taupe pantsuit and matching heels. All the women looked very put together except for one who was in overalls similar to Rachel's. She also skipped in front of the pantsuit woman with a huge smile on her face.

Locks had arrived while she'd been chatting with the girls. Rachel couldn't hear what the Franks sisters said to the cousins as they walked in. Too many people chatting and the coffee machines were loud.

There were three younger girls with the five older ones. Rachel guessed they were triplets because she couldn't tell any difference between them. Jesse talked with them, pointing at Locks. The three grinned, walking over, and Rachel strained to hear what they said.

"Are you our Great-Uncle Noah?" one asked.

Locks stared at them. Gunner leaned close. "Noah is Locks' given name," he said softly.

"I guess I might be. Is your grandfather Aaron Franks?" Locks asked, his voice shaking.

"Yes, but you look a little kinder because you're smiling," one of them said.

"Beck, that's inappropriate," one of the women said. She walked toward Locks, holding out her hand. "This is Beck, Taylor, and Regan, my daughters. I'm the youngest, Naomi," she said.

"Pleased to meet you. Two sets of triplets?" Locks asked, staring at the other sisters who'd walked in. Now that Locks mentioned it, Rachel could see the three were triplets, though their hair color and cut were all different, as was their hairstyle.

Jesse led everyone over. "Dad, I'd like you to meet Tori, who is the oldest. AJ is next, then the triplets are Lilah, Chloe, and Naomi."

Rachel wondered what all Locks was thinking. He nodded, stood up a little straighter.

"Seems like we've got some Franks cousins to get to know better. You all have a place to stay tonight? My wife, Hope, and I have plenty of rooms at the house," Locks offered.

"I have an extra bedroom at my house," Beth chimed in.

"Me too," Sarah said.

"We'd planned on staying in Dodge City, but if you have room for us here, I'd love the chance to get to know you. When Jesse contacted us, we had no idea our dad had a brother," Tori said.

Locks chuckled. "I'm not surprised. He didn't exactly approve of my life or the position my wife occupied in our bail bonds company. He cut all ties and I was a hothead. I got mad that he didn't think I was good enough and decided to never contact him. Prideful, I know. Let's get you ladies some snacks because Broken Hearts Brewing has some amazing food. Do you like to read? I'd love to buy you some books because isn't that what Great-Uncles do?" Locks said.

His words seemed to relax everyone, and in minutes, they had pushed a couple of tables together and were all eating.

Rachel really wished she could go sit close to listen, but duty called. She gave Gunner a kiss on the cheek before hurrying to Clara and Faith over by the cats.

"Are these going to be available all the time?" Faith asked.

"Yes, as long as I can keep them in stock. Why do you ask?" Rachel said.

"Well, I love the names and the idea of gift boxes. I can see using these as teacher gifts or friend gifts even for girls Deborah's age. If they'd be available, I was going to start making my list," Faith said.

"Yes. For now, they are only available in the shop, but we're going to add shipping so that people can buy them for gifts. We'll have a Broken Hearts Brewing box that will include a book and one of the cats, possibly a coffee mug," Rachel said.

"You have done a fantastic job. I'm so happy you came to Bluff Creek. I consider you family, so get ready for me to spoil my new grandkids," Regina said.

Rachel giggled. "You mean that hadn't started yet with all the deliveries we received?"

"Oh, that was just the start. Let me know if you need anything. I'm going to go tell the kids how much I love the cards they made," Regina said.

Rachel left Faith picking out cats. Rachel had left some in the back room for their actual opening day but just from seeing how many were being sold, she'd need to get started making some more. She was ecstatic everything was going so well. Tomorrow evening was their restocking time before they opened for good, bright and early Valentine's morning. Gunner had made heart cookies with a ribbon on them with Broken Hearts Brewing's name. Rachel was glad he'd put some in the freezer to keep because they were addictive, and she couldn't leave them alone.

CHAPTER NINETEEN

Rachel breathed deeply, concentrating on putting the last couple books on the shelf. The store was quiet. Night had fallen, with only the streetlight at the end of the block on outside. She and Gunner might want to add some outside lights under the pink and red awning—maybe some Edison lights hanging from underneath it.

The coffee shop that seemed so welcoming during the day gave off sinister vibes tonight. She needed a couple more of the kids' cards to refill the station for tomorrow. She pulled them from her stock area in their office and walked back out.

"Well, well, well, looks like beanpole found a cushy spot. If you want to keep those bratty kids, I think five thousand would be a good start to our payment plan," Maynard wheezed.

The last year hadn't been kind to him. His unwashed, greasy hair hung past his ears. She cataloged him for any threats. She couldn't see anything she deemed a threat unless a seventies tracksuit, which had numerous stains, could carry some dread disease.

"What? Your sunny personality can't figure out an answer? How about you bend over that chair and I'll do you for free for old times' sake? Then you get your scrawny, stupid ass over to the register and give me my money!" Maynard screamed.

"It is I, Prospect Finn, tasked with fighting for the rights of majestic unicorns. How may I be of service to the realm?" Finn asked, walking in from the kitchen.

"I take it Gunner is through waiting?" Rachel asked, grinning.

"He was fine to wait if you wanted to have your say but since you weren't talking, he was concerned," Finn said.

"Who are you, and why do you have a pink unicorn backpack?" Maynard asked.

Gunner walked out, followed by the rest of the men who'd wanted to support her. Beth and the sisters had offered but with the cousins in town only through Saturday, Rachel was good with just the guys.

"He's one of us," Gunner said.

Oh, her man looked good with his black short-sleeve T-shirt under his cut. She'd told Gunner last night about the plan she'd put into action with Beth. Instead of being irritated, he'd praised her for taking the initiative and asked how he could help. When he'd held her in his arms and said he had a fierce need to protect her while letting her have closure with Maynard, she'd been glad they were alone, and she'd crossed one other thing off her bucket list with Gunner. Her man loved her mouth on him.

"Who's us?" Maynard asked.

"The Bluff Creek Brotherhood MC," Finn replied.

"Well, she owes me money," Maynard said.

Gunner's warm hand on her shoulder reminded her that Maynard had no power over her.

"Babe, this is your plan. What do you want?" he asked.

She thought about this a lot in the last twenty-four hours when she realized that she could have whatever she wanted.

"I want him to sign away his rights to the kids, and I want him to sign the divorce papers. I don't need to do anything to him because if he signs, then he's no longer a factor in my life. Now, if my man and his friends want to teach Maynard a lesson or two before he's run out of town, then I'll let you know that he's left-handed just in case the lesson starts before he signs the papers," Rachel said, enjoying the look of disbelief on Maynard's face.

"I believe we can make that happen," Gunner said.

"Okay," Rachel said, tugging Gunner down so she could claim his lips. This man and the way he lit up her body was something she was going to cherish the rest of her life. She pulled away, staring into his eyes.

"Come to our bed when you're done. I want to wake up beside you before we open the store. I'll let the kids know tonight that you'll be staying over," Rachel said. The smirk on Gunner's face told her exactly how they'd be celebrating her divorce.

"Okay, Baron's going to run you home. I want to know you're safe with the kids," he said.

She nodded because honestly, what else was she supposed to do when her big, tattooed biker wanted her safe?

She glanced at Maynard, a shudder running through her when she saw he'd already peed his pants. Ugh.

"Maynard, I better never see you again," Rachel said, taking the arm Baron held out to her.

"Take me home, please," Rachel said.

"My pleasure, darlin'," Baron replied.

Gunner waited until he saw Baron and Rachel drive by in her van. He didn't want any of this to touch his sweet woman, who oozed sunshine. Come to think of it, he didn't really want any of this to touch the shop or have them clean up before tomorrow.

"Now, what are we going to do with you, Maynard? I'm guessing you're not going to just sign away your rights to the kids and sign the divorce papers, are you?" Gunner said.

"I want some money," Maynard said.

"Hey, since obviously he might need some convincing, my wife suggested we use the boxing area in the gym. Concrete is sealed for easy cleanup and they are already closed," Bear offered.

"Umm, I like that idea. Did your wife also suggest a way to get him there because urine boy isn't riding on the back of any of our bikes," Gunner said. They'd parked their bikes down the street at Bluff Creek Ink and gone in the back door of the shop to hide three hours before Maynard had shown up.

"No, she didn't," Bear replied.

"I suppose the town might get irritated if we hooked a rope to his hands and made him run behind our motorcycles until he fell," Stone said.

"I am so glad Roam had you come to Bluff Creek," War said, chuckling.

"Maynard's chariot awaits," Rascal called from the back of the building.

Gunner had Finn grab one arm while Gunner grabbed the other. Once they had him outside, Gunner chuckled.

Rascal had one of the side-by-sides, but he'd hooked up the deer sled that the club used during deer season.

"I thought we could tie him down in the deer sled," Rascal said.

"Won't the deer sled get torn up on the highway?" Finn asked.

"If we head over one street, there's only Bremerton land between here and our compound. I called Jake and told him we had a little situation. He was more than happy for us to drive across his land," Rascal said.

"I want to help drive," Gunner said.

Rascal shook his head. "It's your right to drive. Lead the way."

Gunner started the side-by-side while Finn and Ben tied Maynard down. Flick jumped into the front seat and Brody in the back. Gunner gunned the side-by-side. As he drove over the hills and maybe a couple cacti, the screams of bad daddy in the back were music to his ears.

It was almost anticlimactic when he pulled the vehicle into the parking lot of the gym. Maynard was begging to sign the papers.

Maybe a better man would have let Maynard sign the papers and be on his way, but Maynard had threatened his own children. Gunner had the guys hold Maynard so he could talk with him first.

"I want to make sure that you understand what's going to happen. You've signed everything. Now, you're going to leave and never try to contact the kids or Rachel again. I don't care if you are down to your last penny and you think maybe the kids will help you. Don't come near them. I'm giving you a gift," Gunner said.

"A gift, like money," Maynard blubbered.

"No, like a gift that I'm letting you live. A man who threatens his son that if the son says something, the man will kill his own daughter and wife deserves to die. You're getting to live. That's your gift," Gunner said, following his words with some satisfying hits to Maynard's face and belly. He wished he could have hit him a little more, but Maynard collapsed to the floor, crying and begging for them to stop.

"I don't care if anyone else wants to get some hits in. When you're done, I want him taken to the bus stop in Dodge City. Buy him a ticket to the farthest stop on the line," Gunner opened his wallet and handed Finn eight hundreds.

"Whatever's left after you buy the ticket, he can have but I want you to watch him get on the bus and watch it pull out of the terminal, got it?" Gunner asked.

"We'll take care of it," Finn and Ben answered in unison.

That twin thing was freaky sometimes.

"Then I'm heading home to the woman I plan on asking to marry me and be my Old Lady tomorrow," Gunner said, heading out of the gym.

One door closed and another was opening for them. Marcus and Chelle would be his to raise with Rachel. He walked toward the house. The gym was only about a seven-minute walk across the compound. He'd use the time to think about how he wanted to propose tomorrow.

He stared at the dark sky with the stars glittering. He had everything he ever wanted. His step was a little lighter as he walked toward home. His home with Rachel, Marcus, and Chelle. Now that they would be a family, maybe the kids needed one or two animals to celebrate.

CHAPTER TWENTY

Rachel sighed as she straightened the table one more time.

"It's perfect," Gunner said.

"Yeah, Mama, I luvs it," Chelle said, grinning, showing off that adorable gap in her teeth.

The kids had been ecstatic when she said Gunner would be staying over. This morning, they'd all been up early. Rachel had drunk an extra cup of coffee because she and Gunner had celebrated last night with a little shower sex. Gunner had said hopefully the water would muffle any noises.

"Mama, it's ten minutes until we open. We need to talk to you," Marcus said.

His voice sounded so serious. She thought both kids were happy about Gunner but maybe she'd missed it.

"Okay, what about?" Rachel asked, not sure she wanted to hear the answer.

Gunner handed his phone to Marcus. Marcus fiddled with the phone until music started. It was catchy but she didn't recognize it.

Gunner got down on one knee. "Rachel, you are the missing piece that I hadn't known I needed. When you came to Bluff Creek, I realized with you, I was whole. And with you came these two amazing kids. I can't think of any better way of celebrating Valentine's Day than by asking you two questions. First, as soon as your divorce is final, will you marry me and let me adopt the kids because you bring the sunshine and smiles into my life?" Gunner said.

Rachel nodded as tears filled her eyes. "Yes," she said.

At her words, clapping and whistling surrounded them. Her Bluff Creek family filed in from upstairs, the office, and the kitchen. She couldn't believe she'd missed them.

Gunner stood up, taking her hand and accepting something from War.

"Well, besides marrying me, I need to know you'll be my Old Lady and ride with me until I can't ride anymore. Will you?" Gunner asked.

"Yes, I want to be with you forever," she said softly.

Feeling the light weight of the leather settle over her gave her that final piece of home.

"Now I can't not have my kids be a part of the MC. Are you both ready to be a part of Bluff Creek?" Gunner asked.

At their nods, he helped them on with their cuts like she'd seen all the MC kids wear.

"Now that I've got my family, let's open Broken Hearts Brewing and help others find the love I have. The shop is already a success because I found you, my sunshine and my beloved," Gunner said, leaning down to kiss her, tugging the kids close to them for hugs.

She didn't care about the catcalls or the cheers at his actions. She was home and that last little missing piece of her heart had been found.

Gunner stared around Broken Hearts Brewing. They'd had record crowds today. He was glad that he, Rachel, and the club had decided that they'd be open Tuesday through Saturday. They could have some time to enjoy being together and get the place restocked.

There were deliveries scheduled for Tuesday morning to replenish their stock. When Rachel had noticed how excited everyone was for the books on February seventh, she'd talked to him about putting another order in immediately. His woman had a great business mind and seeing the picked-over shelves, he was thankful for her thinking ahead.

The kids hadn't wanted to leave today. When they'd gotten a little tired, Rachel had set them up with a movie in the office on the couch. Bear had said the diner would deliver their supper this evening. Gunner was thankful for that because he had one less thing to worry about tonight.

Brody walked in, "Hey Gunner, you need to come see this."

Gunner nodded. "Morgan, I'm heading outside. Yell if you need help."

Morgan smiled. "We're good. Dad is coming by, and if we have questions, I'm sure he can help."

Gunner followed Brody out back. "What's up?"

Brody walked across the parking lot to where it was darker. He bent down near a bush and pulled out a flashlight. Gunner crouched down beside him.

"Are those puppies?" Gunner asked.

"Yep, our shelter isn't open yet and I can take them if needed," Brody said, pausing.

"But?" Gunner asked.

"You have a new family, and those kids want a pet. This just seems like it was meant to be. I can't tell for sure until we get them out of there, but it looks like a mama dog and two puppies. If you don't want all three, I could take them. Up to you," Brody said.

Gunner stared at the mother. He wasn't sure what she was, but her coat was matted, and she looked a little thin. He pulled his phone out and called Rachel.

"Hello," Rachel said.

"So, Brody brought me out back. There's a stray dog. She's got mats all over her and she has, from what we can see, at least two puppies. Do you…"

"I'll be right out," she said, hanging up.

"What did she say," Brody asked.

"She said she'd be right out and hung up," Gunner said.

"Hmm," Brody murmured.

The dog didn't seem scared of them. She didn't growl or go to move herself or the puppies. He wondered if she was just too tired and hungry to bother with them.

The back door opening had Gunner turning. Rachel came out carrying a basket, the kids following behind her. When they were about ten feet away, he heard Rachel admonish the kids to remember what she said.

Chelle got on her knees and scooted close to where Gunner was. Marcus crouched down by Brody. He had a couple pieces of hot dog.

"Mama said you found us pets to celebrate our family and Valentine's Day," Marcus said.

"I guess I did," Gunner said, grinning at his sunshine.

"Now, she seems fine but why don't you break apart the hot dog and toss a piece close to her? Did you all bring a bowl with water?" Brody asked.

Rachel handed the bowl and water bottle to Brody.

"This is the best Valentine's ever," Chelle said.

Gunner crouched in the parking lot, watching his family fall in love with a scruffy matted dog and her puppies, and he had to agree. This was the best Valentine's ever. Between the hot dogs, the cheese Chelle had, and Rachel's soft voice cooing to the dog, in less than thirty minutes, Mama dog and puppies were in the basket, safely ensconced in the back of the van. The store was closed, and he was on his motorcycle ready to follow the vehicle holding his heart home. Marcus waved at him from the van as they pulled out.

Gunner needed to get some small helmets so he could take the kids on a ride. He and Brody pulled out to head home.

He'd come to Bluff Creek wanting to find a job and a home. He'd found so much more. Brotherhood. Family and the piece he was missing. He wasn't sure how he could top their first Valentine's together because they'd opened the store, gotten engaged, and added some pets to the family. He might have set the bar a little high for Valentine's Day.

Thank you so much for reading The Biker's Beloved. If the people of Bluff Creek have you wanting more. I have a free prequel available here: https://BookHip.com/FZBFJND It also subscribes you to my newsletter. If you're on Facebook, you can also join my VIP reader group- Nat Logan's Bluff Creek Beauties.

14 Days of Love & Lust
Team Bikers

Liberty Parker – Shot through the Heart

Marteeka Kaarland – Blood and Valentines

Nat Logan – The Biker's Beloved

Ember Davis – Mayhem's Heart

Quinn Ryder – Loving Voorhees

K.L. Ramsey – Love to Hate You!

Darlene Tallman – Stupid Cupid

Michelle Dups – Igniting Red's FLame

Jessa Aarons – Cupid's Double Shot of Whiskey

Lacy Rose – True Love and Tailpipes

Nikki Landis – Chrome & Kisses

Winter Travers – Fueled by Desire

14 Days of Love & Lust

Team Mobsters

Elle Boon – Hunting Starla

Calia Wilde – Valentine's Code

Chelle C. Craze – Devious Devotions

D. Williams – Bloody Rose

Annelise Reynolds – Sweet Deception

Naomi Porter – His Dangerous Duty

Rae B. Lake – Steamy Night & Deadly Sins

Morgan Jane Mitchell – Valentine Vendetta

Glenna Maynard – Bullet for my Sweetheart

Jade Royal – Beautiful Ruin

Lila Grey – Claddagh and Carnage

Amy Davies – Romeo's Deal

E.C. Land – Heart of the Kingpin